PLAY MAKER

KING OF THE COURT #3

PIPER LAWSON

Content editing by Becca Mysoor
Line and copy editing by Cassie Robertson
Proofreading by Devon Burke
Cover design by Emily Wittig

*For anyone
who's had to play
the long game*

NOVA

This isn't happening.

Half an hour ago, we were at the gala celebrating the team and my mural.

Now, Clay's moving to LA.

Rain streaks the window, and I wrap my coat tighter around me even though we're in the car. The headline replays in my mind. I could pull it up again, but I don't have to. Those words are emblazoned in my mind.

**TRADE RUMOR CONFIRMED:
DENVER KODIAKS FORWARD CLAYTON WADE
SENT TO LA IN MULTIYEAR DEAL FOR KYLE
BANKS**

"It's going to move fast from here." Clay's voice has me looking toward the driver's seat.

His bowtie is still fastened, the tattoos snaking up his neck and out the cuffs of his tux. His hair sticks up from the hand he shoved through it after getting in the car. He sat there for thirty seconds staring into space before starting the engine and pulling out of the stadium garage.

"How fast?"

His phone buzzes with alerts between us, the screen lighting up every second. He flips it over. "I need to call my agent and go see Coach."

"It's eleven at night."

I feel him watching me, gauging my reaction even as he's dealing with his own.

"I'm not getting any sleep. Doesn't mean you can't." He pulls up in front of the condo building and takes my hand.

He drops a key into my palm. "I'll see you later."

I shift out of the car, disbelief washing over me as I race to the doors of the building. I love an adventure, but this one feels like a game where everyone can keep up except me.

Six months ago, I was living alone in Boston unemployed after my cowardly ex ran away in the night.

Now, I'm in Denver and moving in with my six-five, tattooed and grumpy all-star pro athlete boyfriend.

At least I was supposed to be.

"Clay..."

I start to turn back, but he's already gone.

I go up to Clay's place and let myself in, kicking off my heels at the door. I turn on the lights and wander around the living room without a destination.

He's wanted a trade to LA for so long. It was his endgame, and I'd almost come to accept that he'd be leaving.

Except...

He told me Harlan had agreed to keep him in Denver. That he wanted it.

It's not clear what this means for us, but I'm desperately afraid I'm going to lose him.

A knock on the door makes me jump. I cross to the peephole. *Brooke.*

"Clay's not here," I say as I open the door to find her still in her gala outfit, no sign of rain on her anywhere, a bottle clutched in one hand.

"I figured. I came for you, dummy."

We go to the kitchen, and I pull glasses I've never used from the cupboards. I pour two fingers in each, and she drops in ice cubes.

"I can't sit down," I say when she glances at the couch.

"Cool. We can walk and drink."

We pace down the hall, and I glance into the room that was going to be my studio. Clay's sports memorabilia are half packed in boxes.

I pause in front of a shelf of trophies and medals. "I've never won anything like that. Mar was always the overachiever."

Brooke laughs. "Between me and Jay, I was the

overachiever. He never tried hard at anything. Not until basketball. Then he had friends, and I never saw him so motivated. He has some of these things, but not like Clay. This is another level."

"Yeah." I exhale hard, not sure I understand it. Or that I want it.

"You didn't know about this," Brooke says.

"That obvious?" I say dryly before taking a sip of my drink.

"You can't fake the expression you had when you read that press release. So, unless you're the world's best actress... it was a surprise to you. Clay, on the other hand, it's not so clear."

I'm not sure how much to say. I want to be candid with my friend, but won't be disloyal to the man I love.

"What was in that one?" Brook nods to a glass case big enough to hold a baseball.

"Nothing. It's always been empty."

"It's for a championship ring," she says.

I never asked Clay about it, but the moment Brooke says it, I know that she's right. "If I tell you the truth, will you keep it between us?"

She squeezes my hand. "Chicks before dicks. Always."

"He wants to win. It eats him up when he doesn't. And with his injury, it's been really hard. Still, he was coming around. He likes being here and his time with the guys. I don't understand what changed."

4

"Management's always working on these deals until the very last minute. Maybe something came up that Harlan couldn't refuse."

"That's what I don't understand. Harlan wanted this too. He believes in Clay and that he can win here." I shake my head in frustration. "Clay didn't stick around to talk to me about it. He dropped me off and went—"

"To see his agent?"

"And Coach," I say. Coach is still in a coma, but I can understand Clay wants to be with him before he leaves.

She nods. "They're going to want him to report to LA this week. He'll be in an LA uniform by Friday. Maybe sooner."

My head spins from the idea of him packing up and moving across the country in a matter of hours.

Brooke lifts her glass in a toast, her lips curving. "This is the lifestyle, basketball girlfriend. Reason number 512 why it's not for me. Question is, is it for you?"

I love Clay, and I love what we are together, but we're still finding our footing. This could change everything.

I hear the apartment door shut, and Clay hollers, "Nova?"

I glance at my phone. It's after one in the morning.

"In here." We stick our heads out.

Clay is already walking toward me, but he pauses when he sees I'm not alone. "Brooke."

"I was just leaving. Your girl and I needed to have a chat. Good luck in LA."

He watches her go.

I close the distance between us, looking up at him. Clay is both alert and exhausted at once. His tux jacket and bowtie are gone, his shirt open at the collar, swirls of ink flirting with his neck. "How did things go with your agent? And Coach?"

"Agent talked more." He kicks off his shoes and crosses the carpet.

We meet in the middle, his hands finding my waist in a way that's reassuring. He's my anchor in this disconcerting storm.

"The deal's done. LA picked up my contract. They were top of my trade list, so my agent never thought about pushing back when it came through earlier today." He pauses. "They're still a favorite to win the championship."

He wants this. He's just shocked by the way it went down.

"That's good, then," I manage.

Clay pulls me close, his arms tightening around me. "I'm sorry about tonight. It was supposed to be your night, and instead it's been a shit show—"

I press up onto my toes and brush my lips over his.

He kisses me back, both comforting and a little desperate at once.

When he pulls away, he says, "They want me in LA tomorrow."

My brows shoot up. "That's fast."

"That's business. Millions on every game. They don't like to wait around."

I shake my head and think about Brooke's words.

"I was going to give that to you tonight." He nods to the key he gave me earlier glinting dully on the kitchen island.

It would have been mine.

And now it's not. This place isn't.

"What can I do?" I ask.

Clay rubs a hand across the dark shadow along his jaw, his eyes swirling with emotion. His grip on me tightens. "You came here for your sister. You have a friend in Brooke. You didn't sign on for this life."

The silence is loud, a buzz that drowns out logic and time. My blood pounds in my veins.

"But?" I prompt.

"But I don't want to lose you. Not tonight. Not like this." He tugs on his hair in frustration. "With you, things are finally starting to make sense. The only time I used to feel right was on the court. You changed that."

The opening in my ribs is like a rush of water released from a dam. Wild and chaotic, unsure of a destination, but crashing forward at breakneck speed.

"I can't promise it will be easy..." he goes on.

His voice is already fading, drowned out by the hammering of my heart.

I've finally started to feel settled in Denver with family and friends.

Except...

A huge part of that is this man.

He's the brightest part of my day, and his hard-won smiles light me up like nothing else. The way he holds me as if I'm the only thing that matters makes me feel for the first time like I do matter.

Like I'm exactly where I'm supposed to be.

My hands stroke up his chest, covering his heart.

"I'd love to come with you."

NOVA

"*I* can't believe you got us in on such short notice."

"It's my job." The realtor flashes startlingly white teeth as she punches in the gate code from the driver's side of her BMW.

"I know you said a condo is fine, but I wanted you to see what a house would look like, particularly given your generous budget. It's furnished with four bedrooms, three baths, a pool, and a half basketball court."

She parks and we get out of the car.

In the time she's been taking me around LA, we've seen two places already, but neither felt like a place I could live. The first was stark and too perfect, like a museum without artifacts. The second was dark and stifling, the high ceilings unable to compensate for the slate finishes.

This one is beautiful, stucco with arched windows and a well-maintained garden.

I strip off my light sweater and tie it around my waist so I'm wearing only a tank top. If I needed a reminder we were in for a change, it hit me the moment I stepped off the plane.

The sunshine warms my face, the palm trees swaying in the breeze.

When we talked about me looking for a rental for us, Clay gave me a budget that made my eyes bug out.

If there's one thing I'm good at, it's making a home when I'm transplanted. We're building something new here, and I want it to feel welcoming from the start.

I pull out my phone to snap a picture, glancing at my texts.

Grumpy Baller: I'm holding your hand right now.

The message from Clay came through before I left on the plane.

I told him I'd fly commercial if only because it's more environmentally friendly. So, he got me a first-class ticket and bought me seats 1A and 1B.

"So you're not arguing with any attractive strangers," he told me.

I follow the realtor inside to a bright foyer with

warm wood floors and light spilling in everywhere. Beyond, the living room is furnished with a contemporary sitting area anchored by a sectional couch that looks as if it could fit an entire basketball team. I'm instantly charmed.

"It's a relatively close drive to the arena," she goes on.

"It's beautiful. I don't know what we'd do here with all this space," I admit as I follow her through the floorplan.

"Have guests? Or kids?" she asks.

"Guests definitely." I smile.

We haven't talked about kids.

We haven't even talked about how long we're staying. Clay's contract has an option this summer that, as I understand it, means he could leave LA if he wants.

This feels like a big leap. The other night at Clay's apartment, it seemed like the only path forward. Now I'm realizing how crazy it was.

The kitchen is updated with warm gray counters and soft white cabinets, and the living room is huge with a vaulted ceiling and a chandelier, wood beams crossing the space. One of the bedrooms would make an amazing studio. It has a huge arched window and the same warm wood floors as the rest of the place, plus soft cream walls.

"I'll admit I'm a basketball fan. I was excited to see the deal go through. Though it's always a gamble messing with a team's chemistry so close to the end of the season," the realtor says as I look around.

"Of course," I say as if I've already considered it at length.

Everything's been such a whirlwind that I haven't.

Though Brooke drove me to the airport and hugged me goodbye, I'm guessing none of the guys have done the same for Clay. Social media is blowing up with rumors about how long this has been in the works and whether this was a betrayal of the Denver guys who'd invested in Clay.

Although he hasn't said anything about it, he must be hurting over it.

Neither Jay's nor Miles's social media profiles have mentioned the trade, not that I expected they would. While they're both still following me, they unfollowed him.

"What do you think?" The realtor cuts into my thoughts.

"I really love it. I want to show Clay." I want him to love it too. I pull out my phone and type up a text. "Could we get back in later today to see this again?"

"Of course."

I want this change to be good for both of us. I'll miss Brooke and the guys and my sister, but I can always visit. I want to do everything I can to make this easy for Clay.

"We used to move around a lot as kids," I tell her.

"When we packed up to move somewhere else, we always brought a piece of it with us."

She smiles. "Like what?"

"Daisies."

The realtor crosses to the bedroom window, pulls back the shutters, and opens the glass wide. She leans out and peers over the sill.

I follow her to the edge and look into the garden below. Dozens of sunny white-and-yellow blooms greet me.

"They grow like wildfire there."

Hope sprouts from between my ribs.

We can do this. I'll make it work for both of us.

3

CLAY

"*T*ook you long enough." The team's GM welcomes me to the arena.

"If I'd come any sooner, I'd still have been wearing my clothes from last night."

He laughs.

This morning, my agent and assistant got the logistics sorted while I packed a couple of bags to get me through the week or two until I get the rest of my stuff sent over.

Nova booked a later flight and volunteered to go apartment hunting.

I still can't believe she agreed to follow me here. I've never had a woman take that kind of a chance on me. As if what we are transcends my wild career.

I want to show her she made the right decision.

The GM takes me through the halls, nodding to staff as we pass. "You belong here, Clay. This is a place for winners. We're after a ring this year, and we've spared no expense to bring you here."

I've played on a few different teams in my career, and every building feels different. This one's like a gilded castle. The arena is full of banners hanging in rows from the ceiling.

Division champions.

Conference champions.

League champions.

Our tour ends on the court, where the team is getting warmed up for practice.

"This is Clayton Wade. As you've heard, we acquired him yesterday in a trade. You'll miss Kyle, but come the postseason, Clay'll be your new best friend."

There are a few nods, but mostly the group is silent and composed.

Fine by me. I'm here to work.

Their point guard, Isaac, steps up and claps me on the back. "Welcome to LA. We'll try to go easy on you the first day."

We line up to start drills.

They'll give me a locker and new stuff, but for now, I'm in Nike.

There are new formations, plays and coverages specific to each individual team. This year in Denver, I've appreciated learning the ins and outs that allow other guys to contribute.

"I'll get up to speed on those soon," I tell one of

the coaches as I sit to catch my breath and watch the others run a defensive sequence.

"Or we'll cut them if they don't suit your style."

Isaac, on the court nearby, overhears. His grin fades.

They have an unfair number of stars, especially with me. They have an A-list fan base—everyone from Tyler Adams to Harrison King sits courtside—and winning with style is what matters.

With that come egos.

No matter how many guys want to be the best, there's only one ball.

I line up again to run the next drill. Isaac comes over to guard me.

"You found a place to live yet?" He asks it so casually I'm not sure he's addressing me.

"My girl's looking—"

Before I can finish, the ball goes up.

Isaac gets to it first, darting past me and taking it to the hoop for a layup. A few guys shout their approval, and Isaac jogs back.

"Sorry, man. Couldn't help it," he says easily.

It's irritating, but I brush it off.

"Today," I finish as we set up again. "She's looking today."

The ball goes up. This time I get it, hitting him harder than necessary as I grab the ball, and take it up the court, flipping it to another teammate to dunk. He nods after, a cool thank-you I return.

"I dunno how you deal with it. Thad"—he nods

to one of the other guys—"was saying how his girl does nothing but complain about all the shit she wants, that he's never home, all that crap. Not cool when you're carrying everything. No way that doesn't affect your game."

It's not straight trash talk, but he's calling me out.

"You're single," I guess.

"Hell yeah. I can think about all that after I retire." Isaac shakes his head as we change to another drill.

I'm not a defensive specialist, but there's no way I'm letting Isaac score. I slide in front of him, setting my feet to absorb the charge as he tries to fight his way to the basket. Isaac's charging six-five collides with my blocking six-five.

I go down hard.

The floor slams into me as I land on my hip and knee. Pain radiates from both joints, and I grind my teeth.

"Defensive foul!" Coach calls.

Isaac appears over me, silhouetted against the lights as he holds out a hand. "Welcome to LA."

On my feet, I walk off the discomfort, refusing to let it show.

"That's practice for today," Coach calls before blowing the whistle. "We have a game tomorrow. I expect to see you all for shootaround. Clay, we'll get you video time with our lead analysts and a meeting to go over some of the coverages."

"You good?" one of the trainers asks me when I cross to the bench.

I nod, ignoring the pain.

Even if some of the guys aren't happy to have me here, we all want to win. As I grab my phone, I see two missed texts.

Nova: OMG, I found the perfect place! Can't wait to show you.

Nova: I'm on my way over.

Her name on my phone makes the knot in my chest ease instantly.

I tug on a hoodie over my jersey only to glance up and see Nova hovering in the stands, halfway up. She's dressed in a denim skirt and a white tank that cling to her curves. Her blond-pink hair falls in waves around her bare shoulders.

When she sees me looking, she waves and smiles, bouncing on her toes.

My lips twitch and I nod back.

Despite the GM's words, maybe I don't quite fit in here.

But neither does she, and I love her for it.

4

NOVA

*C*lay always looks good after practice. Exhausted and invigorated, like he just slayed a dragon.

Or his own personal demons.

He meets me in the hallway after showering, his hair still damp.

"Did you show them how to play?" I ask.

Clay wraps an arm around my waist and kisses me until I'm breathless. If I'm surprised by the urgency, I don't show it. I kiss him back, pressing up onto my toes as his mouth slants across mine.

I want to be his anchor. The one person he looks for, smiles at.

We're in the middle of the arena, and I'm suddenly wishing we were in private.

"Didn't realize PDA was still a thing," an unfamiliar voice says from the other side of Clay.

I look past him at another guy in a hoodie.

He's vaguely familiar, but I can't place him. There are too many players in the league for me to remember all of them, but I vow to memorize all the LA guys this week if it kills me.

I smile and extend a hand. "I'm Nova."

He glances at it before shaking it, his mouth curving. "Isaac. This is a big move. Nice of you to drop everything for Clay. You got friends here? Family?"

"They're back in Denver." I feel Clay tense at my side, but maybe it's my imagination. "I'm excited for the opportunity. We both are." I take Clay's hand and squeeze.

Clay's already tugging me toward the door.

"That was weird," I murmur as we head for the parking garage.

"No shit."

"I meant you. You don't like him." I cut him a look as we reach Clay's rental.

"It's not about liking everyone. Sometimes you just have to work with them." He unlocks the doors.

I shift into the car, dismayed. "You guys will be teammates, right? You have to get along."

He looks at me a long time, then sighs.

It feels as if he's pulling away, but I brush it off. He's had a wild week, he's probably exhausted.

"You're going to love this place." I punch the address into the GPS, and we start through the city.

Even though this house is only a few miles from the arena, it still takes us twenty minutes to get there.

We punch the code in at the gate, then pull into the driveway and get out.

"This is it."

The realtor sent me the temporary door passcode this afternoon, and I punch it into the keypad. Inside, I watch Clay for his reaction.

He surveys the walls, the floors, the decor, walking slowly through the main level.

"What do you think?" I ask, suddenly nervous. Maybe I got a weird read on his taste. I want him to love this.

"Tell me about it."

I spring into action. "So, the kitchen..."

I talk him through the details as if I'm the realtor.

The vaulted living room. The original floors and arched windows.

His eyes warm more and more as we pass through each room.

We go to the second bedroom, where I say, "This could be a studio."

"Keep talking."

I show him the view from outside, the flower garden and daisies.

"We're missing one room." Clay's voice is gruff, but there's a softness under the edge.

"Are we?" I feign ignorance. But with a smile, I lead him to the final door. "This is the primary bedroom. There's a huge ensuite. A king bed. Scratch that—a California king."

"Seems pretty big." He comes up behind me and wraps his arms around me.

My head tilts as his lips skim down my neck. "It has to be. For sleeping, I mean. Professional athletes need lots of rest."

He drags me closer, fitting his hard body against my back, my ass. My eyes drift shut as I feel him getting hard.

The realtor might've been a basketball fan, but this fantasy is my life.

"Thank you for the two first-class tickets," I murmur, covering his hands with mine.

Sunlight streams in the window, surrounding us with bright light, and I want to stretch like a cat. Especially when his hands move over my body and slide up under my tank top.

"You're welcome. Any hot strangers on the plane?"

He plays with my nipples, which harden despite the heat. His touch sends pleasure shimmering along my nerve endings.

"What would you say if I said yes?"

He pinches one of my breasts hard enough to make me gasp.

Clay spins me, lifting me. I wrap my arms greedily around his tattooed neck.

"I'd remind you that you're mine."

Normally, he's more relaxed after practice, but today, he's wound tight as he sets me on the windowsill. The yard behind me is lined with hedges, separating it from the street beyond.

He leans a hand on either side of me. In this position he's still a foot taller. The swirls of black ink along his arms and neck twine together as he flexes.

"Nothing has to change here," I murmur. "It can be exactly like it was in Denver."

"It won't be anything like Denver," he replies. "The city. The team."

I sigh. "Not even you and me?"

Clay rests his forehead against mine.

"Sure, there are no mountains or snow. But what if different is good?" I suggest, and his gaze narrows. "If LA is hotter than Denver, maybe LA Clay and Nova are too."

His mouth twitches. "Hotter, huh?"

"Mhmm." My gaze drags down to his gray sweatpants, the bulge that seems to swell with every second. I grasp on to the windowsill. "What's the hottest thing I could do right now?"

Clay ghosts his lips over my ear, his voice borderline feral.

"Take me out," he rumbles.

I'm breathless with anticipation as I reach for the waistband of his pants, feel the silken head of his huge cock.

I want him to like the house, but right now, I want *him*.

"Now what?" I ask, all innocence as I run my hands around the girth of him.

Clay's breath is shallow. "Suck."

He's so wide, and while I've played with him lots, I've barely been able to get my lips around him, not to mention give him an actual blowjob.

He's never seemed to care.

Now, more than anything, I want to make him feel good.

I bend forward, my tongue darting out to lick the underside.

His muscles tighten, and his low growl rumbles through me. "Fuck yes."

The words spur me on. It's a challenge, and I seem to like those lately. The muscles in my jaw ache as I work him in my mouth with both hands.

It's awkward.

It's also beyond sexy.

The pressure of him against my tongue has saliva coating his shaft. I start to move up and down, my fingers barely encircling him.

Clay strips off his shirt, never taking his gaze from me as he arches to press deeper. "Dammit, Nova. You look so beautiful sucking my cock."

I squirm on the windowsill to get more comfortable, or as comfortable as I can, then go back to my work.

His other hand reaches for my hair, and he tightens his grip in the strands. The next second, he pushes me down farther on his cock. I gag, but it's worth it for the way he spasms in my mouth.

He's so gorgeous, his hard body covered in tattoos and flexing in the sunlight through the window.

I'm greedy for him.

This time, I take him farther, his cock bumping against my throat while I manage not to choke on him.

I figure out a rhythm, guided by his hands but not constrained by them. I speed up when I want, add a little flourish of my tongue around the head of his cock.

But when I take him deep again, he grunts and pulls me off.

"What's wrong?" I gasp.

"As much as I want to, I'm not coming in your mouth, because I need to fuck you." Clay slides a hand up my skirt and inside my panties. "You'll be a good girl and come on my cock."

With the next thrust, two of his fingers slip inside me.

Soon he's pumping me, his thumb pressing on my clit.

"That's not your cock," I gasp helpfully.

"You can come on my fingers first," he replies, every bit as helpfully.

I'm already tightening around him, ripples of ecstatic pleasure gripping me until I'm a mess of aftershocks.

He pulls his fingers from me, then strips off my tank top.

I take a second to admire his beautiful body, the hard lines of muscle and the tattoos that mark him everywhere. Clay lifts my hips and drags off my skirt and panties in one movement.

"Seems as if you're getting used to this LA business," I suggest, trying to ignore that I'm half naked in the window.

"It's growing on me."

This is probably not what the realtor had in mind when she said we could come back today.

"We're supposed to be looking at the house," I tease, twisting a piece of hair around my finger.

"Need to make sure it's sturdy." His gaze runs over me hungrily before coming back to my eyes. "Hold on."

To what?

But I grip the sides of the window for balance as he lifts my knees until they're pressed against my ribcage. He positions himself between my thighs, stroking my wet pussy with his cock.

Ohhh.

Clay grabs my hips with one hand and sinks inside.

My body stretches to fit him, the feel of it making me gasp.

We're reflected in a mirror on the other side of the room, his incredible ass flexing as he sinks into me with a relentless rhythm.

We move together, me gripping the windowsill with one hand and him with the other. There's a good chance I'm about to fall into the garden.

It'd be worth it.

"I'm close," I whisper.

His face is pressed close, his dark eyes bright with hunger and need.

"You're so sexy when you come," he rasps against my mouth. "So fucking hot, the way you trust me."

Does he mean physically?

I don't think so.

At least, not only.

I squeeze and I'm lost.

Pleasure crashes into me like a riot of colors and textures playing together in unexpected and gorgeous ways.

Clay groans as he stiffens inside me. In the mirror, every muscle in his back and ass and legs clenches as he comes. He's art, a damned renaissance sculpture, only he's filthy and real.

When we come down, I realize we've made it to the floor. He's under me, protecting me from the wood.

"Thank you," he murmurs into my hair.

I don't think he means for the blowjob.

His fingers thread into my hair, brushing it away from my sweaty face. There's so much tenderness on his expression.

"Think the house is sturdy enough?" I ask.

"Might do the trick."

His slow grin makes my heart skip.

"I haven't even told you about the daisies."

The next two weeks pass in a blur.

The house came furnished, but I've been setting up our belongings and ordering things we need.

Clay had most of his things shipped from Denver.

I buy some new art supplies using my money from the mural and arrange the ones he got me in the room we decided would be my studio.

Plus, I paint the entire house. He said we could hire someone, but having a roller or brush in my hand makes me feel more myself.

At Clay's first home game in LA, I'm introduced to a couple of other wives and girlfriends. They're nice, but they remind me of the Kodashians back in Denver—only more tanned with sleek waist-length hair, body-skimming outfits, and heels so high I'd need an insurance policy to wear them.

The team gets a win, but there's not the same excitement within the team as when Denver wins. It feels more like an expectation coming to reality.

Or maybe the chemistry isn't there with LA.

Yet.

It's not there yet.

The next afternoon, I take a break from painting to turn on the TV. I've just watched a few minutes of Denver playing Boston out East when Clay comes in the front door.

"The place looks good," he comments, crossing to the couch and dropping a kiss on my head.

"Yeah? I was thinking I should work on the

gardens next. They need more color. Which reminds me. I need to get my hair done." I found a few places to freshen up my pink strands.

Clay reaches for his gym bag and pulls out an envelope.

"What's that?" I ask as he passes it over. I rip it open to find a black credit card with my name on it.

"I have a credit card."

"Yeah, but this is on my account. Don't argue," he starts before I can.

"You might regret this. When was the last time you gave a woman access to your bank account?" I tease.

"Never." The seriousness on his face makes my chest squeeze.

"Thanks," I murmur. "I'll try to resist pulling a Julia Roberts and buying up Rodeo Drive."

"If it makes you smile, I want you to."

Gahhhh.

He glances toward the TV and does a double take. "Why're you watching that?"

"I wanted to see how our friends are doing," I say as he sits next to me, making the massive couch sink under his weight.

On the screen, Denver is scrapping intently. Jay and Rookie, Miles and Atlas, plus a new guy who came as part of the trade with LA.

"Rookie's gotten to the free throw line three times since I turned the TV on, and he made all of them."

"Oh yeah?" I hear the humor in Clay's voice as his lips brush my ear.

I smile too. "Mhmm. And Miles has been good from three. Jay's still trying to figure out schemes with the new guy."

"I see." Clay reaches an arm around my waist absently. "You think you know everything about basketball?"

"Some things," I agree, and he chuckles. "It feels weird, watching them from a distance. When was the last time you talked to the guys?"

"The gala."

My mouth falls open. "You haven't talked to any of them? Even by text?"

He shakes his head and heads toward our room. "At the end of the day, it's business."

He's away on the East Coast for two games when I call Mari.

"How are you feeling?"

"I'm still craving cheese. I blame it on the baby."

I laugh.

"I have sono pics. Want to see?"

My mouth falls open. "Of course!"

It takes a minute for my phone to buzz, and I hurry to click into the black-and-white image.

"Oh my God. The baby is perfect."

She snorts. "It's a bean. You can't see anything yet."

"No, I totally can. It's got a huge brain. And an even bigger heart," I insist as she laughs. "And everyone will love them so much."

Mar's quiet for a minute but finally sighs. "I hope so. How are things for you and Clay?"

"We're figuring it out. I'd never say it to Clay, but I miss Denver."

At night after the games, Clay calls and we talk for an hour. I ask him about each game, but he steers the conversation to what I'm doing, or the city he's in, or how the house is. We end up having phone sex, and I fall asleep in the California king bed, my body humming from the long-distance orgasm and ocean of space beside me.

During the days, I've been painting in my growing studio. I got so used to painting the mural every day that it feels strange not to have that be my focus.

The money from the commission is sitting in my account, but there's been limited interest since the gala. If I want to make a career at this, I need to keep working.

On a morning walk, a billboard for a modern dance performance stopped me in my tracks. I went to see it by myself that afternoon and was swept up in the artistry of it.

Over the next three days, I paint the dancer. I pull from my memory and from supplemental images

I find online. As the sunlight streams into my studio, I draw and paint, and my heart feels full in a way it hasn't since coming to LA.

Brooke comes to visit for a weekend while Clay is on the road, and we go for dinner and shopping and to Huntington Beach and to see a show.

As we head out of the theater, I say, "Can I ask you about your brother?"

"Miss Denver enough you want to date him instead?" she replies dryly.

I laugh. "No, I mean about what happened when Clay left. I didn't expect it to cause such a rift. Clay says it's only business, but I don't believe that."

More than that, I don't believe him. That it's nothing personal for him. Clay misses those guys. He might even feel responsible for what happened. But he won't talk to me about it. We're spending more time alone together than we ever have, but he's even more of a mystery.

"Jay understands how the league works. He's been in it as long as Clay. But it's a weird system. As an influencer, I decide who I work with and when and for how much. I choose my partnerships, and I can end one for any reason. If I'm exhausted, I can take a break.

"But as a pro athlete, they pay you enough money and you stop being a human. You're a god, but you're also a commodity. A rare, expensive one, like a diamond. Everyone around you worships you, but it's all about getting the most out of you until you're used up—the most points, the most endorsements, the most cash. People buy and sell you, trade you and show you off, and expect you to be grateful because it's done by the rules of the player agreement, and at the end of the day, you have a house in Malibu and three ex-wives to show for it."

I arch a brow. "That's a very specific example."

We head down the street, through the crowds of well-dressed Californians, sunglasses on their heads and sandals on their feet.

"My brother is loyalty first, the job second. There've been times in his career he could've gotten ahead at the cost of someone else, but he didn't do it. Chances to make more money and sell his soul, but he won't," Brooke says. "When we were kids, our mom always said, 'None of it's worth it if you can't live with yourself.' He took that to heart."

We stop at a corner, waiting for a light to change. "I wish Clay could square things with the guys."

"Distance makes it hard."

"But they're coming to town next week."

An idea grabs me, and I grin at my friend.

Brooke's eyes narrow. "What are you planning?"

5

CLAY

"First game against Denver," Nova calls as she shifts into the car Sunday morning.

"I shouldn't be eating pancakes. They kick my ass, it's on you."

Nova arranged to go to brunch before the game to help me relax.

I've been anticipating this game since I got to LA. It's going to be intense. Always is after a big trade. Players on both sides want to prove their new team won out.

"It must be conflicting. If you win today, Denver's season is over."

"That's the way the league works."

"But sometimes it sucks."

I shake my head. Her plain statement reminds me she's younger than me and doesn't have to put on a face for the media. I appreciate and envy it.

The past couple of weeks have been an adjustment, but she's been a rock. Getting our new place together, holding shit down when I'm here and not, feeling like my home when I'm not sure where that is.

I turn into the parking lot of the brunch restaurant and pull into a spot. I hit the brakes harder than necessary when I see four familiar figures head inside.

Jay, Miles, Rookie, Brooke...

My chest tightens.

"What did you do?" I ask under my breath.

"They're your friends," she insists. Her hand squeezes mine.

I turn to take in her expression, those wide blue eyes and full, pleading lips.

"They're guys I played with," I correct. "I have a new team, and that's where I've got to focus."

"That's crap." Her even reply makes me blink. "At the all-star game, you told me you have friends across the league. Don't let bad blood keep you apart."

Hurt and self-disgust rise up. I haven't told her I reached out to Jay the week of the trade.

He didn't answer.

Probably because he blames me for what went down. He believes the rumors that it was my plan all along.

And wasn't it?

This was always my plan. I deserve whatever Jay

thinks of me. I was the one keeping secrets, the one who put myself above everything.

But I can't tell Nova any of that because saying it out loud will only make the shittiness more real, make me question the decisions I've made.

"They know I'm coming?" I ask.

"No. I had Brooke make the reservation for brunch. But I'm sure they'll be happy once they find out."

Through the window, I see them shift into a booth, smiling and laughing.

Part of me wants to go in there.

But I'm a few hours away from a game that will clinch our playoff standings. A couple of months away from what I always wanted: a shot at a championship.

I can't be hanging out with the Kodiaks.

Nova's hand lands on my shoulder, her touch light but insistent. "Come on, Clay. Just for an hour."

"I have a game to win. You staying or going?"

Her face scrunches up, her expression filled with confusion and disappointment. "I'd like to eat brunch with my friends."

She arches a brow, and I huff out a breath.

"I'll catch up with you later."

She gets out of the car, and I drive off.

Nothing grounds me like a win.

The fire of competing, the thrill of victory—it's all a reminder of why I work my ass off.

My reward isn't only triumph.

It's the clarity that comes with it.

The black and white of knowing what you did was right.

The game has a one-o'clock start. The arena's full as always, with a sprinkling of Denver fans. During warmups, I cut looks at my old team. Jay doesn't meet my eyes, but Miles nods to me.

Rookie grins. "Your girl bought me lunch," he calls as I shoot toward our basket, the ball swishing through the net.

Of course she did. I rub a hand through my hair as I turn back to him. "Only you?"

"Would've been rude if she didn't offer to get it for the other guys too."

I shake my head and wave off the offer of a ball from one of our trainers.

Rookie comes over and fist-bumps me.

"Heard your free throw shooting's improved," I say.

"I get a lot more of 'em with you gone."

My lips twitch. Maybe seeing the guys won't be as bad as I thought and we can still be friends.

"Wade!" one of the trainers calls. This time, I grab the ball when he sends it sailing my way.

"You're better off," I offer.

Rookie shakes his head. "Wouldn't go that far."

His half smile makes me feel guilty again.

At the start of the game, the Kodiaks starters are introduced, then our starters. I line up opposite Miles. The ball goes up, and our team gets it.

They're overmatched by our star power. That's clear in the first five minutes as we rack up basket after basket.

At one point, I look up into the stands at Brooke and Nova cheering side by side in different jerseys and feel the pang of regret.

They make it look so easy. Guess it is when friendship is all you have, no sports or loyalties to come between you.

Kyle, the guy who was traded for me, stops at my side. "I see why you stuck it out in Denver so long," he says, following my gaze to Nova and Brooke. "You know all the hot girls."

The team rivalry is sidelined, my only focus the man in front of me.

"That mouth is going to get you in trouble."

"I was thinking more about hers."

My hands fist at my sides.

I'm not big on giving people the benefit of the doubt, but I'd like to think I'm a better person thanks to Nova's influence.

Plus, I'm on a basketball court with cameras and millions already watching. My options are limited.

"You know that's Jay's sister."

He lifts both hands. "My bad." Kyle seems surprised, like he thought he was making small talk, but when he sees how seriously I take his words, anger creates a predatory glint in his eyes.

In the second quarter, a switch flips and Denver digs in. We play back and forth, scrapping for every possession, every point. I try to take the ball more, but so does Kyle. It ends up being a battle between us instead of between the teams.

And Denver is benefitting. Slowly, they claw their way back.

In the second half, I tell myself to get back to business.

We focus and start to stretch out the lead once again.

When Jay takes a hard foul from Isaac, no one's there to help him up. So, I hold out a hand. He's forced to take it but doesn't say a word.

I'm guarding an inbound play when Kyle leans in and says, "Think I changed my mind. I'd take them together or apart. That pink hair would look real good wrapped around my hand."

I hit him.

My knuckles connect with his cheek, hard enough I hear the crack.

The entire stadium erupts in gasping and hollering. Kyle comes back on me, and I fall hard on my knee.

Pain radiates down my shin, stabbing like a white-hot knife. When I look up, Nova and Brooke are watching with their hands over their faces.

"You're out of the game!" the official declares as I lie on my back, staring at the lights.

I watch the rest from the treatment room as our head athletic trainer probes my knee and calls to arrange scans.

LA wins.

We're bound for the playoffs with prime seeding against our first-round opponents.

Denver is eliminated.

The win doesn't feel nearly as good as I'd hoped.

LA WINS CHAMPIONSHIP
WHILE WADE WATCHES

After sailing through the Western Conference, LA beats Miami to claim the ultimate victory. All-star Clayton Wade watched from the bench nursing a repeat knee injury.

WADE SKIPS SUMMER LEAGUE WITH NO COMMITMENT FOR THE SEASON

Clayton Wade hasn't exercised his player option to stay with LA. Neither has the all-star committed to another team. Is Wade taking a well-deserved break, or is there something else going on?

WITH THE PRESEASON A MONTH AWAY, CLAYTON WADE HAS YET TO WORK OUT FOR ANY TEAMS

It's nearly basketball time again, but the only place Clayton Wade has been photographed is the golf course. What's his plan? Fans drafting their fantasy teams want to know almost as much as the real sports execs.

6

NOVA

September

"*R*elax. See how deep you can take it."

The tension up my thighs intensifies, but I try not to resist it.

My eyes shut. I exhale and bend farther, my nose grazing my knees.

The barre class is full of eager students ready to do whatever the toned, middle-aged instructor says.

"Deeper, baby," a woman with blond hair whispers to the red-haired woman next to me.

The red-haired woman snorts.

"Imagine there's a line connecting your heart to your legs."

"There is. It's called a blood vessel." The blonde again.

This time, the redheaded woman's shoulders rock, and a laugh escapes. She turns toward me, grinning as her bright blue eyes meet mine. She looks vaguely familiar, but it's the humor on her face that makes me bite my cheek.

"If you're going to be disruptive in class, I'm afraid we'll have to ask you to leave." We all straighten as the woman leading the barre session gestures to the group. "Right, everyone?"

Her eyes land on me, and I shrug. "I thought it was funny."

The teacher's penciled brows slide up her forehead as she points at the door. "Out! All three of you."

We bolt for the changeroom, heads down, in a silent line.

Inside my locker, my phone is showing one new text.

Dee: I have offers on the table, and I've used every excuse in the book. Please use whatever magic you have. I'm begging you.

I didn't realize things had gotten this out of hand.

I start to type out a quick text to Clay but get interrupted.

"Sorry, that was my bad," the redheaded woman says to me, and my gaze snaps up.

She's pale and freckled compared to the usually

tan people I've come to recognize in LA but strikingly beautiful. She and her friend look around my age, maybe a few years older.

"Still have half an hour. Think coffee will have the same strengthening effect as barre?" she goes on.

"On your brain," the blonde supplies, and they both laugh.

My lips twitch too.

"I'm Annie," says the redhead, "and this is Elle."

"Nova." I push the hair from my face and lower my phone.

"Why don't you join us?" Annie asks. "The least we can do is buy you a drink after getting you kicked out of barre."

It's better than trying to decide what to do about the fact we're weeks from the start of the season and Clay has no contract and, evidently, isn't speaking to his agent.

The three of us head down the block to a nearby café. The ever-present sunshine beats down, and I tug my sunglasses out of my bag and slip them on my face. It's instinct after the past few months here.

"This place has the best lattes. I'd sell my appendix for one," Annie says as she holds the door for me to go in first.

"That's hardly a sacrifice. No one needs their appendix," Elle counters.

"My liver?"

"That one you do need."

"I love this place," I say. "I draw in here sometimes."

"Are you an artist?" Elle asks as we line up at the counter behind another pair of women talking, little dogs clutched in their arms.

It's the first time someone's asked me that in a long time.

I pull out my phone and show them my social feed.

Annie scrolls, her eyes widening, and Elle nods slowly.

"This is amazing," Annie says as she surveys the posts of dancers, athletes, kids playing. "Is this why you've been taking barre, to study dancers?"

"Annie's a dancer. A real one," Elle volunteers, and Annie rolls her eyes. "And a singer and an actor and a writer."

"Elle's exaggerating."

We're ordering our drinks, Annie pulling out a credit card before I can even offer to pay, when suddenly her face clicks in my mind.

"You're Annie Jamieson."

She's the daughter of one of the biggest rock stars the world has ever known, and she's married to another of them. She also sang the national anthem at one of the playoff games in LA this year.

"I heard you were amazing on Broadway. I hope you're returning someday?"

"I'm on a stage break since my daughter's two. I almost miss the days of eight performances a week."

We laugh as the barista prepares our drinks.

"I don't have kids, but my sister is due any day with her first. A girl." Excitement bubbles up as I think of the sono images Mari's been sending me— from the first one of a tiny, hard-to-make-out form to the latest, which was so distinct I could imagine reaching out to touch her and having her wrap a tiny fist around my finger. "It's hard because she's in Colorado. I'm still hoping to be there for the birth, but things have been complicated here."

As in I have no idea where we'll be living until Clay decides what his plan is.

"You had a lot of basketball in your feed. You must be a fan," Annie says.

"My boyfriend plays."

"Pickup?"

"For LA."

Annie nods knowingly as she takes her drink and leads the way toward a corner table in the window, turning her back on the street. Maybe to get the sunlight or the privacy.

These two remind me of my friends in Denver. They're not impressed by people who are "A Big Deal," either because they are too or because they just don't give a fuck about labels and follower counts. Which a relief because I have a hard time guarding against people who are.

"It was so great when they won this year," Annie says. "I follow a little, and we sit in one of the boxes from time to time. Which one is your boyfriend, if you don't mind my asking?"

"Clayton Wade."

They exchange a look.

"It must have been hard to watch his team win from the sidelines. But he still gets a ring."

"True. I just wish I knew where he was going to be next year," I say.

"He doesn't have a contract?"

I shake my head, feeling foolish.

"Negotiations are always hard," Annie says kindly.

We moved here for basketball, but Clay hasn't talked to me about his career since championships.

I sip my latte—it is good—and try to ignore the unease that's been the dominant feeling in my stomach for weeks.

Annie picks up her phone, types away on it, then hits a button with a flourish. "There. I'm one of your bazillion followers." She grins. "Tyler and I are having a party this weekend. You should come. It's less exercise than barre class, but I can promise stellar beverages. Some of them a little harder than what's in here." She taps the wall of her mug.

My chest expands with hope. It feels like I haven't found a rhythm since the championship. Since we moved here, really. The prospect of new friends is energizing.

"Thanks for the invitation. I'll talk to Clay."

"If he doesn't want to come"—Annie flips her hair—"you should come anyway."

CLAY

"I'm going to destroy you," I inform the guy standing next to me.

"Impossible. You can't beat that."

I line up my shot, eyeing my target. Shift my weight. Pull back. And swing.

Crack.

The golf ball launches toward the horizon.

My three companions watch the arc of the ball. It lands in the center of the fairway.

"You need a backup job, this is it." Tony, a software entrepreneur, claps a hand on my bicep.

We shift into our golf cart, me in the driver's seat, the other two guys getting in theirs. Our caddies look after our bags as we take off toward the fairway.

We finish putting and talk about summer vacation. Everyone seems to have spent theirs in Greece or at their lake houses.

"What about you?" one of the others asks me.

"You kidding? He's on every billboard in town," Tony declares.

Since we won the championship, I've been booking more endorsement deals than ever.

Ironic seeing as how I didn't contribute a single point in the postseason.

But people's perception matters more than the truth.

"Can we get a pic?" Tony asks as we finish up our eighteen holes.

After I agree and get in the shot, he takes off his ball cap, turns the phone camera toward us, and clicks.

"I'll text it to you," he promises.

My phone buzzes for the tenth time.

"You need to get that?" Tony prompts.

"Nah."

Except when I glance at the phone, it's Nova.

Nova: Dee texted me about your contract.

Fuck. Dee's persistent like that.

Clay: She shouldn't be bothering you.

Nova: Seems like she's doing her job. What time will you be home?

Clay: Not sure. There's a dinner after.

I sit at a round table and make small talk I used to hate and drink until the buzz takes up residence in the back of my brain.

I'm on my third beer when a familiar face approaches.

"Hey, man. How's it going?" He's one of the young guys from the LA team. I clap him on the back, and he does the same to me. "It's been a wild ride, right? Can't wait to get my ring. Bet you've been dreaming of it for weeks. I know I have."

When I sleep, I can't seem to dream of anything.

That's the problem.

I put on a good face, act like the guy who's a champion.

None of it felt the way it was supposed to. There was no rush of satisfaction, no fulfillment that I've achieved my lifelong dream.

I got to the top of the mountain and found nothing there. Only the conviction deepening each day that I didn't earn it.

And I have no idea what to do with that.

I head for the doors without saying goodbye to the organizers. My car stays in the parking lot as I get into a limo and it pulls away.

Tony sent me the picture. When I look at it for the first time, it takes me aback. He looks comfortable in his green polo. I'm wearing sunglasses and a black polo, my tattoos patterning my arms.

Is this who I am now?

There are options—teams that would sign me if I wanted to stay in the game even on the chance my knee doesn't come back. But I hate the idea of being some kind of favor, a legacy whose only contribution is some kind of aura of championship, like stale cologne that aged badly.

I could announce my retirement, but that future is even more bleak.

The fence swings wide, and the limo pulls toward the house. It's dark, the outside lights by the gate unlit.

"Let me drop you at the—" The limo pulls to an abrupt stop midway to the door. "I'm sorry, Mr. Wade. I think I drove into your garden."

There's no mistaking the squish of tires on the turf as he backs onto the asphalt once again and navigates around the plot of flowers Nova added in front of the house this spring.

I'm not ready to go in.

Alone, I don't have to lie about the way I feel.

Doing it in public is one thing, but pretending to Nova is a different kind of hard.

"Wait here a second," I tell the driver as the vehicle comes to a smooth stop.

"Everything okay, Mr. Wade?"

I don't answer.

I love Nova and I used to anticipate seeing her at the end of the day. Now I'm not sure I remember how to look forward to anything.

It's like I'm separated from the world by a glass wall.

There are little bottles of alcohol lining the shelves in the mini fridge, and I grab one.

"Mr. Wade, I hate to ask, but could I get an autograph? It's for my son."

The hope in his voice makes me pause. I set the bottle back on the shelf and take the hat and marker he passes through.

When I get out of the car, I drag my feet up the driveway and hit the entry code for the house.

Lights are on in the living room. I'm heading for the bathroom when I see the door to her studio is ajar.

Inside, Nova's painting at her easel. Soft music streams from a Bluetooth speaker in one corner.

Her hair is blonde, streaked blonder from the sun, and twisted into a messy knot on her head. There's none of the pink left, and I try to remember when that happened.

Her gray cotton dress reaches her knees. Bare legs and feet are tanned from a summer outside.

Nova's focused on her easel, but she's swaying too.

I imagine her eyes lifting to mine, grabbing me in that way she has.

Me crossing to her.

Turning her in my arms, carrying her to the wall, and pinning her there.

Her legs go around my waist. She reaches for my belt, unfastening it and my pants. We get them off, and I press between her legs, sliding in all the way. Her back arches as she moans softly.

Neither of us says a word.

For a moment, it's everything.

For a moment, it's enough.

As if feeling my attention, her eyes lift from the easel. "Hi."

I blink from the doorway. "Surprised you're up."

"I couldn't sleep." She stretches her arms overhead, revealing spots of paint on her arms and neck.

Around us are canvases everywhere, mostly images of dancers.

"You don't do basketball anymore," I notice.

"That makes two of us." My body stiffens, and her eyes widen at the same time. "Sorry. I just mean that it's September and we have no idea what you're doing next year. Where you're playing or—"

"I'll figure it out." My voice is rougher than I intend, but it feels as disconnected from me as every other part of my body.

"How was the tournament?"

"We raised a lot of money." *I feel empty.* "How was barre class?" I ask, pushing to remember her schedule.

"Good. I made friends who invited us to a party this weekend. Want to go?" she asks.

A party.

I just spent all day acting around other people. But she wants to—I can tell.

"Yeah, sure."

She looks as though she wants to say more but doesn't.

"The limo drove through one of the gardens," I go on finally.

Her face screws up. "The daisies?"

"Maybe." I lift a shoulder. "Good night."

"Night."

Halfway out the door, I glance back...

But she's already painting again.

7

NOVA

"*C*an you get Tyler Adams to sign my tits?" Brooke demands through the speakerphone.

"His wife invited me. That would be awkward." I dust powder on my cheeks in the bathroom. "Besides, how would I even do that?"

"You're right. Get him to sign your tits and send me a picture."

"Not happening," Clay says as he walks past the door, buttoning his shirt.

My lips curve as I stare after him.

It's the first time I've heard him make a joke in days.

Weeks?

Since we arrived in LA, things haven't been the same between us. Clay tried to tell me they wouldn't be, but I was convinced I could make this place a home for us.

Somehow the harder I tried, the more distant he became.

LA winning the championship only seemed to push him further beneath water. He withdrew, going from quiet to resigned and grumpy to disconnected.

He's been down since the season ended. I wish he'd get a therapist, but since we moved to LA, he hasn't found one in state.

Maybe I've been going about it the wrong ways, trying to keep him connected to his old friends and teammates.

Maybe what we've needed is to make new friends together.

"Also, I saw your sister going for lunch with Chloe yesterday," Brooke continues, bringing me back. "She looked round and happy."

"Perfect. I'm still hoping I can make it there in time for the birth."

"When's she due?"

"Two weeks."

"You better get moving," Brooke warns. "She looked ready to pop."

I hang up with my friend, put my makeup away and fluff my hair.

Half an hour later, we're parking on a lush, curved street in the Hills.

"Hey," I say to Clay when I grab my purse and shift out, "if anyone asks about your plans for next year, what should I say?"

He stiffens slightly it's almost imperceptible. "Same as always. Nothing's finalized."

I want it to be finalized for *us*. Still, Clay told me he'd called his agent back. I feel as though things are getting better and we might be turning a corner.

Now we're walking up the pathway to the huge white house surrounded by a high hedge of green.

Clay's wearing jeans, a white polo, and Jordans, his tattoos mellow against his tan skin. He looks every bit the Californian. I'm in a white sundress and wedge sandals, and I styled my hair in waves.

Music drifts from the back of the house or the inside—or both. Clay takes my hand and leads the way.

When we get to the front door, Annie's already there, her arms wide. "Nova! You're here!"

She looks effortlessly cool in a gray knit strapless dress that skims her body, gathered high on one hip and brushing her toes on the other side.

"Barre girl!" The blonde, Elle, shouts from inside.

"Welcome." If Annie's intimidated by the enormous guy that is my boyfriend, she doesn't show it. "Tyler's around here somewhere."

We follow her inside, where a few dozen people are already mingling, a few dancing, everyone with a drink in their hand. Annie cuts through the crowd to a dark-haired guy in a Henley. Her hand rests on his shoulder, and she murmurs something in his ear.

He looks over, dark eyes piercing both of us.

"Don't even think about the tits thing." Clay's hand tightens on my waist.

Annie motions us over and introduces her husband, Tyler.

"Rose is staying with my dad and stepmom tonight, so it's only adults. God, do I need a night of only adults." Annie's laughter sounds like tinkling bells at a holiday concert. "Can I get you both a drink?"

We agree, and she retrieves a beer for Clay and a spritzer for me. We talk with Tyler and Annie, and they introduce us to a few more friends: a reality-TV star, a British entertainment magnate; his wife, who's a world-renowned DJ; and his brother, who's a professional soccer player. Ash—the soccer player—and Clay get started on the difference between pro sports in the UK and the US.

"I have a confession: I also needed some girl time," Annie confides in me, leaning in. "My dad's been visiting, so he and Tyler talk shop all the time. It's too much testosterone, and Rose isn't old enough or loud enough to back me up yet." She winks and tugs me out to the patio, which has a pool and a sweeping view of West Hollywood.

Annie Jamieson is remarkably down-to-earth for someone with 270 degrees of ocean outside her kitchen. I like her already.

"I get what it's like to be surrounded by boys working," I say. "I left most of my friends behind in Denver when we came for Clay's work."

She nods sympathetically. "An opportunity comes up and you don't have time to think. You leap or you fall. What they never tell you is even when you say yes, it's not all it's cracked up to be."

I take a sip of my drink, staring at the sunset. "Are you allowed to say that?"

She bursts out laughing, a hand covering her mouth. "Jesus, Nova, it's a good thing I don't drink champagne. I'd have bubbles coming out my nose for weeks." Once her laughter fades, she says, "You're right. Once you get all the things, you're not allowed to say shit. Even if what you wanted doesn't feel as good as you thought it would."

My gaze scans the party, landing on Clay talking to Tyler and the entertainment magnate. Harrison, I think his name is.

"So, how do you deal?" I ask.

"You make friends. The kind you can be honest with." Her gaze lands on a dark-haired woman weaving through the crowd.

Little Queen. The DJ. She played one night in Denver when we all went out.

Annie wraps an arm around the woman's neck and drags her close. "Tell me you weren't fucking Harry in the hall closet again."

"I thought that was reserved for you and Tyler," the woman deadpans, her eyes sliding between us. "At least at parties."

Annie gasps. "How did you know about that?!"

"Everyone knows about that."

Annie laughs and turns back to me. "Rae and I went to school together. Elle too."

"Nova," I say, holding out a hand.

Rae takes it with a secretive smile. "The boys are entertaining themselves." She glances at them. "Tattoos. He with you?"

"Yeah."

"Good. They just started talking about American football. They'll be occupied a while."

I take another drink, enjoying my new friends.

"Are you and Harrison together?" I ask.

She lifts her hand, a huge yellow diamond on her finger. "He swears we are. I remember nothing."

"Rae's the only one who could keep Harry in line," Annie informs me. "The bigger the ego, the bigger the ego slayer needed."

"So, does that mean Tyler's humble?" They exchange a look, and I keep talking. "Because you seem really sweet, I mean."

Annie grins, her gold eyes glinting.

"That man would crawl for her. In fact, I think he has," Rae drawls.

"What about you and Clay?" Annie asks.

Between the vibe we have and the alcohol, I feel safe telling them the truth—at least part of it.

"When LA won the championship, I thought everything would be easy."

"And it wasn't," Annie finishes.

I shake my head. "We used to talk all the time. But it feels like he's shut me out of his head. I wish he would decide what he wants to do next year." I flash a smile, realizing I'm opening up too much. Even if these women are discreet, this is a party and I'm being a downer. "At least I can work from anywhere, so if he picks a different team, I'll be ready."

"Nova's an artist," Annie explains to Rae. "And a really talented one."

Annie pulls out her phone and clicks over to social media.

After looking through some of my pictures, Rae says, "She should do your premiere."

Golden eyes widen.

"What premiere?" I ask, confused.

"A's in a film coming out next month. It was supposed to be some small indie thing, but it's getting rave reviews. They want a collection of portraits of the actors for the opening."

"You'd be perfect," Annie insists. "The director tried to pull it together before, but some things fell through."

"That sounds incredible. I'd be grateful if you put me forward."

"It's not putting you forward," Rae drawls as Annie types on her phone. "There'll be an email in your inbox in twenty-four hours."

Five minutes later, my phone dings with an offer.

My chest expands with hope. This is for me, it's within my control, and it has nothing to do with Clay. I feel as if I've stumbled across a tiny gem I wasn't looking for.

That's when another message comes through.

Harlan: Mari's in labor.

My stomach flips.
I text back immediately.

Nova: OMG! How is she doing? Are you heading to the hospital?

Harlan: Already there. Pushing now.

I use the washroom and bump into a figure on the way out.

"Hey." Clay catches me.

I gaze up at him, tipsy. "Mari's in labor."

"Shit. That's early."

The way he says it hits me like a wrong note.

"Only a few days," I respond. "I'm a little sad I couldn't be there."

"You could've gone."

My mouth falls open.

Someone comes down the hall to use the bathroom, and I step through an open door into what looks like a guest room.

Clay follows, half shutting it behind us.

"I needed to be here for *you*," I say quietly enough my voice doesn't travel into the hall.

His frown says I'm being difficult. "I'm a grown man, Nova. You don't need to babysit me."

"It's not babysitting, it's choosing where we're going to live."

"Maybe I won't sign anywhere."

My throat closes, frustration battling with helplessness.

I used to tolerate feeling like the world called all the shots. There are times, like with the trade to LA, when you have to roll with it. But this feels different.

The curtains in the bedroom are drawn to keep it from overheating in the sun. It lends to the impression that this conversation is secret.

"You won't open up about what's going on with you, for months now," I say, breaking the silence. "I know you got hurt, but you've been injured before. This is different."

Clay rubs both hands through his hair. "I didn't make you come to LA."

"I know. I thought we could be happy here," I whisper as I reach for his wrists. "You got everything you said you wanted. The team. The win. The legacy. There's a ring with your name on it they're going to hand you at the first home game of the season. If you know what will make you happy, tell me. Let me in."

He pulls away, pacing the floor beyond me. Still close, but out of reach.

"I don't need help. I need the right offer."

He's mentioned that there are a few potential

offers and the teams but not the details. This is the first time he's been under contract negotiations since we've been together, and I guess I thought I'd be a bigger part of that.

"What does Dee think?" I ask.

"She just wants to get paid."

Clay rubs a hand through his hair, his gaze going anywhere but me. It's a habit lately, and I hate it. But when his attention returns to my face, I almost wish it hadn't.

"The problem isn't that I'm not happy—it's that you *are*," he says. "You like it here. You can do your art, make your friends, and it doesn't fit with the shit going on in my head. You're bright and rainbows, and I'm a storm, and you're trying to make me something I'm not."

It feels as if he's slapped me. The truth of it hits me hard enough I take a step back.

When my phone buzzes, I pick it up to silence it, but the image on the screen accompanying the text makes my mouth fall open.

There's a photo of a tiny pink baby clasped in my tired, smiling sister's arms.

I'm longing to be with them, to smile and laugh and fawn over the baby. At the same time, I'm devastated that I missed the chance to be there.

Mari: She's here :) Now what do I do?

Her words are an invitation, and a lifeline.

I didn't realize how much of my life I've been putting on hold these past months while I waited for Clay to make a decision he's no closer to making.

One it seems he has no intention of letting me into.

The pain in my chest intensifies until it's hard to breathe. I lift my face to take in Clay's impassive expression.

"Maybe we should take a break," I hear myself say.

I expect him to drag my face up to his, to kiss me until I can't breathe, let alone speak.

Or to tell me it's impossible to have space from someone you swore you were the same person as.

"A break from what?" His voice is so low I almost think I imagined it.

I'm the one bringing up the problem that's been between us for weeks, months, but somehow, I feel more helpless than ever.

"From us? From pretending everything's good when it's not? From going through the same pattern every day and living in limbo?"

I'd take angry Clay. Hell, I'd even take hurt Clay because it would mean I can still hurt him.

As he nods to the door, waiting for me to go first, I realize numbly that I won't get either of those.

And that hurts the most.

8

NOVA

"*S*he likes you." Mari drops into a chair outside on the patio behind the house.

I sigh. "I like her."

I adjust Emily on my lap, bouncing her gently in the way I've learned she prefers over the past two weeks.

"Keep her," my sister offers.

I look over in surprise to see Mari watching, a half smile on her face.

"You're only saying that because you didn't sleep last night. Besides, I'm the cool aunt. I'll dye her hair and drive her to parties and all the things you won't do."

"Not until she's at least sixteen," Mari says.

"Ten," I whisper.

Emily blinks up at me with her big, blue eyes. She's so beautiful, with her perfect fingers and fingernails and dark hair.

"I can already tell she has Harlan's determination. And my stubbornness," Mari says.

"Those are the same thing."

She sticks out her tongue.

It's a gorgeous fall day, the breeze rippling through the trees and cutting through my sweater, and Emily's wrapped cozily in her sleeper. I wish we could stay like this for hours, the three of us.

I lift Emily and pace the patio.

"You want to have kids?" my sister asks.

I bite my lip. "Maybe. At the right time and with the right person."

"But not Clay." She latches on with the precision of a surgeon.

I look over my shoulder at Mari, adjusting the baby in my arms. "Enough with the hard questions."

He and I haven't talked except for a couple of texts since I left.

I said I needed a break, and he's been observing it perfectly.

Too perfectly.

Mari snorts. "Does he understand how lucky he is? For every talented player who busts their ass, there are a dozen just as good who don't make it. Who never get to play in the championship finals. Harlan would kill for what Clay has. He enjoys being a GM, but he misses being a player. It's the consolation prize."

"Clay can't see the lucky part right now."

She shrugs. "He's a selfish man, and guys like that

don't change. Don't hate me." She lifts both hands. "I'm saying it as someone in your corner. You wouldn't have come back if things hadn't fallen apart between you in LA."

"They didn't fall apart," I correct, though I'm not entirely sure what I'm correcting. "We both needed space."

"For how long?"

Until I recognize the man I fell in love with.

Until I know what I should do next.

On some level, I wish he'd rush to my side and say that I was right and he knows what he wants and we can be happy. Because when he wants something, he won't let it go.

He didn't agree to the break, but he didn't try to stop me either.

I might be more relaxed, but dammit, I'm still left wondering what's going on in his head.

I'm just doing it from a distance rather than up close.

"Stay as long as you want," Mari continues when I don't answer. "We love having you around."

Before I left LA, there were times when it felt like living with a stranger.

Only it hurt more because the stranger was someone I loved.

But I couldn't make him happy, no matter how I tried.

Here, I'm needed. I'm important. I matter.

Mari's invitation feels good, but at the same time, I can't hide out here forever.

Can I?

I have to work on the portraits I promised Annie Jamieson's studio. Still, I could start on that here.

"I need my painting stuff from LA. I could go get it. Or ask Clay to send it."

"Get someone else to send it for you. Then you don't have to deal with whatever mood he's in."

I bite my lip. I do feel better since I came here. More relaxed, more grounded.

I glance toward the house. "When does Harlan usually get back from the office? I could make dinner."

"He'll pick something up. And he's been coming home early to take over. He misses her when he has to stay away."

I've managed to mostly avoid spending time alone with him since getting here. Though my sister and I are on more stable ground, I still feel betrayed by the way Harlan handled things with Clay.

As if on cue, the man in question appears, a takeout bag at his side.

"You brought tacos!" Mari sighs. "I love you. And now I know you love me."

"Love is ground beef and house-made tortillas?" he prompts.

"Today it is."

Harlan crosses to his wife and drops a kiss on her forehead before turning back to me.

"Let me help you." I pass Emily to her father and take the bag before following him inside.

"Busy day?" I ask for something to say.

"We're getting the roster organized for this year. Trying to fill gaps and manage expectations."

"You mean James's expectations."

He shifts Emily into one arm, grabs a bottle of wine, and pops the cork. He gets two glasses from the cupboard. The ease of his movements reminds me he played professionally once. He's coordinated and graceful for a guy who wears a suit to work now.

"I'm sorry for what happened with the trade. I really tried to get Clay to stay. James had his own ideas." Harlan slides a full glass over to me. "But it seems it worked out for the best. Clay got his championship."

"I'm not sure it was for the best." I take a sip of wine, the smooth red dancing over my tongue. Harlan will never be my closest confidant after how he handled things with Clay and with me, but I need his input. "He hasn't signed anywhere. He doesn't want to play. I'm worried about him."

My brother-in-law bounces the baby in his arm, ignoring his wine. "You're not wrong to be concerned. Back in college after the truth came about around his girlfriend's relationship with another man, he played Final Four like a machine. At first, I thought perhaps he was coping extraordinarily well. But later, it became clear he wasn't."

I don't pretend to multitask. All my attention is on Harlan.

"At the ceremony, he didn't smile once. He withdrew. We didn't see him for weeks. He shut out the team, his friends. He wouldn't let anyone be there for him."

I think of what's happening now. "What got him out of it?"

Harlan sighs. "That I can't answer. I wish I could."

I set the plates on the island hard enough they clink loudly before opening the takeout bag. "You should have tried harder."

Emily stirs, and Harlan rocks her in his arms before looking at me.

"Doesn't work that way, Nova. He has to want to save himself."

9

CLAY

*I*t's incredible how the days blur together when you don't need to go to work, or work out, or be anywhere for anyone.

In the unrelenting schedule of pro sports, there's no time left to ask why.

Why play basketball?

Why even get up in the morning?

Or is it afternoon?

Nova left seventeen days ago.

Our argument at the party came out of nowhere, yet somehow it felt inevitable.

A break, she called it.

But it's more than that.

I've been left before. I should've known it wouldn't work out. The second I wasn't at my best, things came crashing down.

Yesterday, it hit home in a new way when she sent for her things.

Now Nova's studio is empty, and so is her half of the dresser.

I blink my eyes open to find myself on the couch in sweatpants. The air tastes like the stale pizza still sitting in boxes on the counter.

I flex, and chip crumbs settle into the ridges of my abs.

Apparently, I ate an entire bag of Doritos while watching reality shows.

The TV is on mute, and there's a news headline about the season starting. LA plays their first game tonight.

In the past ten years, I've never not started a season.

It should feel liberating. Instead, it's as if the glass walls are pressing down on me, stifling me, but I can't bring myself to press back.

I spent my entire life trying to be the strongest. The fastest. The best.

Now, I'm nothing.

On the corner of the coffee table is the journal Nova made me last Christmas, made from fabric with a dozen of my tattoos replicated in her steady hand across the surface.

I crack the front cover, folding it open to the first blank page.

It's empty.

Like me.

The sound of a car door outside pulls me to the window. My knee that, during playoffs, screamed

77

every time I put weight on it now functions with barely a whimper. I look out over the driveway and the garden with tire tracks through the daisies.

At the gate, my sister is stabbing at the keypad.

I yank open the door and step onto the mat in bare feet.

"What's your gate code? I tried 'baller baller bills' already," Kat calls.

I give it to her, and a minute later, the car pulls up the driveway.

My sister emerges with a huge handbag in tow and big, round sunglasses. Daniel shifts out of the driver's seat with a wave, and Andy bursts from the back and makes a beeline for the basketball hoop.

Kat crosses to me, eyeing up the garden as she passes. "Can't decide who looks worse, you or the flowers."

I rub a hand over my jaw, remembering I haven't shaved in days. My hair might be long too.

"Kidding. I love you no matter how much you look like a bridge troll."

"What are you doing here?" She hasn't been here since the move—busy with school—and she had to pick the worst time.

Kat wraps an arm around my waist. "We wanted to see you get your ring."

But despite the surprise visit, seeing her always softens the ice in my chest.

I help Daniel bring in the suitcases and put them in the guest room past the door to Nova's studio.

"Do you have a basketball?" Andy demands when we've finished.

"Let me see." I go to the hall closet and rummage through until I find one.

"Who the fuck are you? You don't know where the basketballs are?" Kat quips as we follow him out.

"Haven't touched one since finals," I say as Andy and his dad go to work on the half court.

"*What*?" my sister hisses. I turn to find Kat standing, her arms folded, in my doorway. "When we were kids, you couldn't make it through the day without carrying one around. You even brought it to the table for meals."

The memories make me uneasy. "I needed a break after the season."

"To play charity golf tournaments? To sit around on the couch?" Her eyes narrow. "And if so... I'll hurt you if you've watched more *Selling Sunset* than me."

Kat was always determined as fuck. Even when she was sick, even when things were hard, my sister was a fighter. She might not have legions of fans, people wearing her name and number, but she's stronger than I am. A better hero for the world.

"Where's Nova?" She looks into the house.

"She's visiting family in Denver."

"Since when?"

"A couple weeks." I rub a hand over my face. "She called to have her art supplies and clothes sent."

My sister leans against me, hooking her arm in mine. "I'm sorry. Did you have a fight?"

No, this was worse than a fight. Nova looked at me like I was broken.

"She was upset about... Lots of things. Wanted to take a break."

"And what did you say?"

"What was I supposed to say?"

She sighs. "Clay..."

"Stop. Don't need you practicing your baby therapist moves on me. Tell me about you."

For a second, I swear she's going to argue, but for once, she lets it slide.

"School is hard. Andy's made some new friends. Daniel's work has been exciting. You wouldn't believe how much drama professors cause, they're worse than any of the Greek houses on campus..."

We stand side by side as Daniel and Andy play basketball. It feels good to think about someone else for a change.

When she's finished, I say, "I'm glad you have them."

"Me too." Her familiar face is brightened by the half smile. "Was it like a crash or a slow burn?"

"Huh?"

"After the championship, the downslide. Was it all of a sudden, or did it take time?"

I inhale. We're outside, but there's not enough air. "Maybe it was the moment we won the championship or the game where I got hurt. Maybe it was the time I called Jay and he wouldn't call back. Or the trade itself. Maybe it was all of them."

She nods. "That was what it was like when I was sick. A little at a time, until there was nothing around me that brought me joy. Did you talk to Nova about it?"

"I tried."

"So that's a no."

I bristle. "She came here for me. She was the bright spot in my life. I wanted to be strong for her. I couldn't tell her I hated everything."

Kat pulls back and looks up at me, her eyes the same shade as mine. "When someone loves you, they can tell."

I saw every time Nova looked at me when she thought I didn't notice. With worry, with disappointment, with sadness.

"She didn't want to be here with me."

"She didn't want to be here with*out* you," Kat corrects. "If you don't like the team here, I bet you have a dozen offers."

"My last contract was six years. The longest anyone's offering is three." I say something I haven't voiced out loud to anyone. "It means they think I'm going downhill. That it's only a matter of time."

"Until your career is over? Or until *you're* over?" she prods.

I rub a hand over my face. "Don't shrink me, Kat. Pretty sure that's against your ethics."

"No way, I get extra credit if I practice on family." She grins. "But for real, you been talking to anyone? Professional, I mean?"

I shake my head.

"I think I'm going backward," I say after a moment of silence. "This is the first year I've gotten offered more money for endorsements than to play basketball. Like the teams think I'm over the hill. I don't have it anymore."

It's insulting that my face matters more than what I can do. I spent all my life being the best, and reaching the top wasn't supposed to feel this way.

"One of these days, your career will be over, and you've never thought about it."

My hand flexes convulsively. "What if all I am is basketball? And that's all I'm good for?"

"What if it is?" she repeats evenly.

By my age, most people know who they are.

Everything about me is tied to a game. One that's given me as much as I've given it.

Problem is, I never took much time to think about what would happen when it stopped giving back.

"Clay!" Andy hollers. "You've got to see my layup!"

"Ever since you gave him that hoop for Christmas, he's been hooked," Kat murmurs to me.

I find a smile, for his sake. "I'm watching."

10

NOVA

"*T*his is harder than barre class," I pant as I follow Brooke along the hiking trail.

"How are the portraits going?" she asks to distract me.

My face screws up. "Most of them are done, but I haven't done portraits before. They could be completely wrong."

"Like... you painted the wrong people?" Brooke quips.

Since my art supplies arrived, I've been working on the portraits for Annie Jamieson's film premiere. It's happening next week, and I'm trying to get the paintings of the stars done on time and to the brief we discussed.

"I can't believe I'm going to a movie premiere," I say as we stop at a scenic clearing and I wipe a hand across my face.

"Because it's in LA or because you've never done anything like that for yourself?"

"Both," I admit.

"Are you going to see Mr. Needs-No-Contract while you're in town?" Brooke takes a long swig from her leopard print water bottle.

"I haven't told him about the gig."

My friend spits out a mouthful of water. "Didn't you get it when you were still in LA?"

"It was right before I left. It didn't seem important compared to everything else going on."

"Whatever you do, don't make yourself small. For him or anyone." She nods pointedly. "Let's keep going. I'm earning nachos."

I tilt my head to look up the mountain. "Maybe you can earn nachos for both of us."

We're both dressed to work out, her in a tank top and leather-looking bike shorts, me in shorts and a Kodiaks T-shirt, a ball cap pulled down over my face and a pink ponytail sticking out the back.

My things arrived by courier from LA. I unpacked the first box but couldn't bring myself to open the second.

Kat posted a couple pics of them at the arena when Clay got his ring. It hurt not to be there, but I'm glad she went. It reminded me of right before they won.

"Which ones?" I held up two sets of dress shoes.

Clay looked up from his phone and tugged out his AirPods. "Huh?"

"Which of these amazing shoes are you wearing to what might be your finals-winning game?" I prompted.

He rolled his eyes. "Don't jinx it."

That night was the finals of the championship. LA was up three games to two, and they had a chance to clinch it.

"You guys and your superstitions," I teased. "Everyone knows you can do it."

"Not up to me."

Clay hadn't played since getting hurt in the Denver game. It sucked. He was in the worst mood he'd been in since I met him. I felt for him, but at the same time, I was thrilled he was on the verge of making history.

There's a reason a roster is fifteen guys and not five. Players need to rest. Others get injured. It sucks, but it's part of the game.

"You helped this team get where they are. Everyone wearing a team jersey did," I reminded him. "Plus, your stats line this year is beyond impressive."

"My stats line?" He crossed to me and brushed a kiss across my forehead. "What is my stats line?"

"Um... fifty?"

Clay smirked. "Fifty what?"

I considered. "Points per game? And fifty assists too?" I added for good measure.

"And fifty blocks and steals?"

"No, only forty of those."

He grinned as he took both pairs of shoes from my

hands and walked past me. I followed him into our room and the giant walk-in closet. My dress was on a hanger. One of the walls had been fitted with a custom shoe rack filled with sneakers, and I got there in time to see Clay grab a pair of Nikes off the shelf.

"You don't have to wear basketball shoes," I said.

"Because I'm not playing, you mean."

We both knew it was true.

"Because there are lots of footwear options," I countered, rummaging through his half of the closet. "You could wear...what the hell?"

My fingers closed on massive rubber feet.

"Flippers?" I brandished the bright purple fins as long as my torso. "Are you secretly a scuba diver and you've been holding out on me this entire time?"

Clay grinned. "Nah, they're from one of my sponsors. Got sent to me as part of a promo." He pointed to the logo on one side.

"Well, you could wear flippers to finals. You'll be the only one in snorkelling chic courtside."

He wrapped both arms around me and crushed me against his huge chest. "Thanks, Pink."

"At least you don't need another surgery." I lifted both palms, the flippers flopping with in my hands. "You can do most things, just not play elite basketball."

He huffed out a breath near my ear.

"If I can't play elite basketball, I don't know what I do."

Brooke's phone rings, breaking into my memories.

"Jay?" she answers, frowning at the spotty reception. "What's the...? I can't hear you." She presses the other hand to her ear, then blinks. "Okay."

She clicks off, laughing in disbelief.

"What?"

"Coach is awake."

I stare at her. "I didn't know people got better after being in comas for months."

"Miracle of modern medicine? A few of the guys are going to see him. Then everyone's meeting at Mile High."

We hustle our butts back down the trail and shift into her Lexus.

Clay. He needs to know about this.

I hit his contact, and it rings until his voicemail picks up.

I can't think of the right words, so I click off without a single one.

"Look who it is." Miles catches sight of us when we walk in the doors of Mile High. "Tour de France Barbie and Camp Counselor Skipper."

Brooke flips him off.

Rookie and Atlas smile in welcome, already in the booth. Everyone looks up as Jay and Chloe come inside, him holding the door for her.

When Jay reaches us, he says, "I had to tell him

we didn't make the playoffs. From the expression on the old man's face, the only person who was gonna die in that room was me."

Laughter has the knot in my chest loosening. Miles and Rookie already have pints of beer, and when a waitress comes over, we order more drinks.

"So, how's LA, Skipper?" Miles prompts me.

I fill him in, glossing over some details.

"Saw he got his ring," Rookie says. "How's he doing?"

The door opens again, and we all look up. Clay walks in, his hand on the back of a woman.

"What the...?" Brooke says under her breath.

He's gorgeous in jeans and a camel zip-up sweater shoved up to his elbows, standing a foot and a half above the woman at his side.

She's pretty. Not like the Kodashians' try-hard kind but naturally, her hair falling in soft waves and her face freckled. They exchange a few words, and she looks at us, biting her lip.

She throws her arms around him. Disbelief rises up inside me, chased with white-hot jealousy.

Nowhere in the "break" did the idea of him cozying up with some other woman enter my mind.

Maybe it should have.

The woman leaves and Clay comes over to the booth, his gaze circling the crew. One by one, they size him up. Except Jay, who doesn't move.

"Hey, man," Miles says, breaking the quiet.

"Long time," Clay says, but his eyes land on me.

Apparently.

CLAY

When I heard about Coach, I jumped on the first commercial flight I could get out of LAX, Kat and Daniel insisting they'd be fine finishing their trip in LA without me. After I landed, I saw a missed call from Nova.

Probably about Coach.

Maybe I shouldn't be surprised she tried to let me know, but I am.

I haven't seen Nova in weeks.

Now, she's sitting between Miles and Atlas with her hair piled on her head, her face and arms tanned from the sun. Her T-shirt sleeves are shoved up over her shoulders. The Kodiaks logo on the front of her shirt taunts me.

For a moment, I'm stunned by the sharp feeling of regret in my gut, along with another emotion I can't look at too hard because it might bring me to my knees.

After so long without feeling, I'm finally feeling *something*.

"Ah, you probably want to sit—" Miles starts to get up so I can sit next to Nova, but her hand clamps on his arm. "Right." He looks between us.

"You heard about Coach?" This is from Atlas.

I shove down the irritation at Nova and Miles and focus on my former teammate. "Yeah."

"How was he?" Miles asks, pulling me back to the present, and the guys lean in.

"Eyes open," I respond.

"He say anything to you?" This is Atlas.

"Not really."

"How you been? Helluva tan," Rookie says.

"Sitting around doing nothing will get you that," Miles adds.

"Winner's tan." Atlas nods.

Nova's only a few feet away, and I'm aware of all of her.

"Clay, you want a drink?" the waitress, the owner's daughter, asks as if I never left Denver.

Jay stands suddenly. "I gotta go. I'm late for some shit."

We watch him head out, banging the door against the frame.

Guess some things change and others don't.

Over by the bar, the waitress is struggling with a tray.

"Thanks," she says as I help her right it.

"How's business?" I ask. On paper, I own just less than half of the place, but I rarely review the financial statements that come through.

"You'd be proud of Dad. He modernized the system back here." She shows me the new register.

"It's faster for customers during busy times and easier for accounting." Her phone beeps, and she swears. "Can't fix everything. Someone left some pallets out in the alley."

"I'm on it."

"Below your paygrade, champ." She cocks her head.

"I'm off the clock, and you have customers."

I head to the alley. I know I've been absorbed in my own stuff these past months—didn't need Kat to put a fine point on my ahead-of-schedule mid-life crisis.

Still, seeing Nova in person, this break feels like an extra shitty idea.

She looks good. Is she really getting what she wants here instead of with me?

I grab a few cases and bring them into the storage room. On my second trip, she's gone from the booth. I push out the door and pull up when I see the flash of pink hair on someone kneeling in the alley.

"What are you doing?"

She straightens to face me, tossing her ponytail over her shoulder. "I tripped over this case and broke a bottle."

"On your way to what exactly?"

She doesn't answer but lifts a hand.

I grab her hand and yank her toward me. There's blood oozing from a shallow slice half an inch long. "Don't move."

I go inside to get a first aid kit before returning to the privacy of the alley.

"How're Mari and the baby?" I ask as I set the kit on a barrel and open it.

"Mari's exhausted, but she's obsessed with Emily," she says.

I take out the gauze and disinfectant. "Amazing."

Nova cocks her head. "Did you just say 'amazing'?"

I ignore her and swipe at the cut. Her blue eyes peer up at me from under dark lashes. Nova stiffens but doesn't move away.

"The ring as massive as it looked? I saw the pics," she goes on.

"It's two pounds. Ideal for pawning to fund a gambling debt or smashing through drywall."

"Never know when you need to do some home improvements."

Despite the tension, our easy banter is there just below the surface.

"You get your things?" I ask.

"Yes, thanks. I needed my art supplies."

Her art supplies. Not her clothes.

It feels less like a dagger.

"I'm doing these portraits on commission for an upcoming movie premiere. It came up the night of the party."

I glance up, surprised. "You never told me."

Because of our argument or because she didn't feel

like she could talk to me about the good things going on?

The wound clean, I cover it with a Band-Aid.

"I tried to call you," she says. "About Coach."

"I had my phone off for the plane ride."

"Oh." She tries to pull away, but I don't release her hand.

She can't be jealous. Not the free-spirited woman who could charm a room with an easy smile.

"You said you wanted a break," I remind her.

"I didn't know it would be so easy for you."

The tightness in my gut springs up. "You have no idea how it's been for me."

"Which is the point," she murmurs as she pulls away. "You haven't talked in months."

I exhale hard and seriously consider grabbing her hand again if only to force her to look at me. "Coach's niece called me before you did. I got on a plane and met her at the hospital. She wanted to thank me in person for helping."

"His niece," she echoes, brows lifting.

"You think I was waiting for you to leave so I could hook up with another woman."

"It's not funny."

It is in my head.

I haven't so much as looked at another woman with interest since I met her. She's it for me.

So how the hell did we get here?

"Nova..."

"Wait." She interrupts. "How did you help Coach?"

"His insurance expired a while ago, but he stuck with me. I was going to stick with him."

Her lips part, eyes widening with compassion and other emotions I want to name but can't.

"I know you don't like to talk about your feelings. But you need to try. If you don't, you'll lose more than you already have." She clears her throat. "About the break…"

Fuck, I can't handle her saying all the reasons it's not working between us.

Not again.

"It was the right move," I say before she can.

She squares her shoulders, chin lifting. "Right."

The door behind me opens, and I turn to find Kyle hovering in the doorway.

"Hey. Didn't expect to see you back in Denver," he muses as he takes me in. "Am I interrupting?"

"No." Nova shifts off the barrel.

Kyle flashes his teeth. "I'm Kyle."

"I'm—"

"Nova. I know." His grin lingers as he surveys her. "I'm Clay's replacement. New and improved."

Like fuck you are.

I don't like how he's looking at her. Not one bit.

I pick up the first aid kit, clenching it in my fingers.

She brushes past me, her scent lingering as she reaches the door.

"Huh. Guess LA wasn't the city of dreams for you after all," Kyle observes.

"Don't even fucking think about it." I grab his shirt and drag him close.

"What? You're worried I took your town, now I'm gonna take your girl?" He flashes teeth.

It's not his town. But he thinks it is.

If he believes for a second he'd have a chance with Nova...

"Kyle?" Miles calls from the end of the alley, and I force myself to let go of Kyle. "We're making this get-well card for Coach. Our old coach, that is. Do you want to sign it?"

He brushes himself off, grinning. "Sure."

Nova was right about one thing...

I have more to lose than I thought.

11

NOVA

"*A* little higher," I say.

I haven't been a stickler for perfection, but today it matters.

The woman lifts the frame an inch.

"Oh my God. That's perfect."

I turn to find Annie Jamieson, her hands clasped and eyes wide, in the doorway of the venue. Her red hair falls in sculpted waves, her body encased in a shimmering silver gown. She's a mermaid.

"You look fantastic," I say.

"And you're a genius." She clasps my hand in hers, the other on her heart. "Thank you for doing this. Especially when I'm going to get all the credit."

Since I flew to LA this morning with the final art pieces for the premiere, I've been focused.

It's the first time I've done portraits for a client, and I'm proud of how they turned out.

But this is a big stage, literally.

Tyler Adams comes up behind Annie. I saw him at the crowded party, but he's more intense like this, in a dark suit with the collar open, the black shirt matching his eyes.

"Aren't they beautiful?" Annie asks him, her eyes moving between the portraits.

"Mhmm. But I'm biased." Tyler half smiles at me, then turns the full force of it on his wife as he drags her close.

Swoon. I miss having what they have. I can forget Clay for a few minutes or even an hour, but this reminder makes me long for intimacy. For the closeness of having another person who has your back and thinks you're everything.

Seeing him unexpectedly in Denver knocked the air from my lungs.

Hearing that he'd been supporting Coach this entire time, knowing that he still cares about *something,* gave me hope for him.

"About the break..."

"It was the right move."

I wanted to talk about it, and instead, he just affirmed it.

Evidently, he's taking it easier than me.

The woman hanging the art taps me on the shoulder.

"We should finish getting ready. Thanks again for the opportunity. Great to see you," I say to Annie and Tyler.

The space is bustling with staff dressed in black,

organizing trays for food, filling champagne glasses, and putting finishing touches on the décor.

I snap a picture and post it to social, which the publicity team already gave me permission to do.

When guests start to flow in, I take a minute to escape to the washroom. I got a message from Brooke earlier telling me to kick ass, and even Mari wished me luck before I hopped on my plane this morning. Another text comes in when I'm about to reach for the stall door.

Grumpy Baller: Good luck tonight, Pink. Blow their minds.

My heart flips over.

"Did you see the portraits? They're so crass." A woman's voice comes from outside the stall.

Another responds. "I heard she was a last-minute stand-in. They had another artist lined up, and it fell through."

"The director likes avant-garde, but this is ridiculous. The studio threw money at them. They would've been better to spend it on more champagne."

Laughter follows, and I'm suddenly lightheaded, as if I hadn't eaten all day. I wait until I hear the bathroom door shut to unlock the stall and step out.

Out in the foyer, ushers are moving people into the theater.

I want to run, but I can't. It would be too awkward. So, I follow their hand gestures and head into the dark cinema. My seat is partway up. The cast is seated closer to the front, dressed elegantly. The men on either side of me are wearing press badges.

When the lights go down, the music and credits starting, my mind goes back.

"She was a last-minute stand-in."

"They're so crass."

I sit in the dark, watching the film and ignoring the way my eyes burn.

The movie is beautiful, but it's hard to focus on it with the criticism playing in my head.

It's not even that they hated me or my work but that Annie took a chance on bringing me in for this and I can't stand the thought of letting her down.

At the end, I'm swept out into the foyer with the others. Industry insiders cluster in groups, drinking and gossiping and laughing. I take snapshots of the art for social.

A few guests congratulate me when I tell them I'm the artist.

Which ones hated it? There's no way of knowing.

I skip the lines of people heading for champagne and duck outside. It's warm in early October, the light breeze lifting the hairs under my up-do.

My phone is heavy in my hands as I stare at the photo I posted earlier of the portraits, back when I was proud and confident.

I click back into my texts and hit a contact.

"Pink," Clay answers.

It's the single syllable that unleashes the floodgates. Silent tears stream down my face.

"How's your event?" he asks.

"Great." I swallow. "Okay, not great. Someone hated my art."

"They're morons," he says evenly.

My mouth works for a moment as I glance around the alley. "You haven't seen the portraits. I only posted them on social, and you're not on social."

"I check yours."

That revelation takes a moment to settle. "You do?"

"Yeah." He sounds caught out, as if he might already regret telling me. "Point is, it's not about you, it's about them. People hate on me every day. Look at a single article, a single post from the team or any of the news outlets. It's full of judgment."

I frown, swiping at my cheeks. "Is that supposed to make it hurt less?"

"I won't tell you how you're supposed to feel. What I will tell you is I've been there."

The moon is full, just visible when I pace toward the back of the alley in my sparkly heels.

This is what it feels like for Clay. Every single day.

For the first time in a long time, I feel as if I understand a piece of him that he hides from the world.

I feel as if he wants me to.

"Where are you?" he asks at last.

"Alley beside the theater."

"You got a new thing for alleys?"

I snort, his warmth contagious even from hundreds of miles away.

"Maybe I do." I bite my cheek. "Where are you?"

My feet carry me toward the street again, the noise of traffic and conversation entering the bubble of quiet that was Clay and me.

"Just went to visit Coach. He'll be out of hospital in a few days."

"You're still in Denver." That knowledge lifts my spirits, though I can't place why. "How long are you staying?"

"I'm not sure. A few days more. For Coach."

"That's great," I say and mean it—both that Coach's condition is improving and that Clay is there with him.

It has nothing to do with the fact that I want to see him again.

I lean against the brick wall, thinking only of the man on the other end of the call. "Annie Jamieson and Tyler Adams are the most amazing couple. I don't know how they survive all the pressure and still seem well adjusted."

"You get their secret, you let me know." I smile, and I picture him doing the same.

He clears his throat. "When are you coming back?"

He means to Denver, but for a second, I imagine he means something else.

"Tomorrow."

"You need a care package for the plane? Say the word and there'll be a bottle of tequila waiting."

My lips curve.

"Thanks. I'll think about it."

12

CLAY

"It's a good offer, Clay. A great offer," my agent says over the phone as I finish my set of bench presses.

"Three years," I say as I wipe off the equipment, then I move over to the treadmill.

I've always used a private gym or the Kodiaks' one, but since I'm still in Denver, I'm using the communal gym in my condo building.

I kept the place because it seemed like more of a hassle to sell it, and it wasn't a priority. But for the moment, I'm glad I did.

A guy wearing expensive workout clothes crosses to the bench press, poking at the plates on either side.

"Twenty a year," Dee confirms.

I hit both the incline and speed buttons at once, the belt whirring as it catches up to the pace I want.

"Even if we both know you're not going to command the max salary, you're still expensive.

Teams don't have enough contract space to sign a player like you with the season already underway. Their budgets are committed."

The gym has a bank of windows with a mountain view on a clear day. It's like a crack of light into the dark place I've been living in for the past few months.

I grimace at myself in the mirror as I run, hitting the up button again so the speed increases until my knee registers a complaint.

"It's also New York. Excellent quality of life. You'd be close to Kat, could visit on the weekends."

"They're not a contender," I point out.

"No one can win every year."

If I take the gig, these could be my final years. They'd be comfortable but not sensational. I'd be trading living on the edge for safety, security.

"I'll think about it." I click off the call, then step off the treadmill and hit the reset button.

Maybe this is how it goes for everyone. Even the brightest stars fade into obscurity with time.

I toss my towel in the bin and head for the door.

Nova calling me last night was a big deal. Not only because it's the first she's reached out since she returned to Denver, but because whether she meant to or not, it wasn't only a phone call.

She needed someone to be there for her. She asked me.

Seeing her work online, I couldn't help letting her know how proud I was. I wanted to let whoever made her feel like shit about her work have it.

The irony is, looking back, I made her feel like shit for the moments of happiness she found in LA.

Back in my condo, I go to the bag I packed when I hurried back to see Coach. It's mostly clothes and essentials, but there was one other item I shoved in the front pocket.

The journal Nova made me as a Christmas gift last year.

I open it to the blank front page again.

This time, the empty space feels a little less like a void and a little more like possibility.

"I'm taking him out for the afternoon," I repeat.

The nurse looks at me hard. "Have him back by five."

"Yes, ma'am," Coach says.

After the workout, I still have pent-up energy, so I bust Coach out of the care home where he's convalescing.

"Get me out of this thing," he mutters as we breach the doors with his wheelchair.

"Nope. You can use it when you get out of the car." I help him in, then pack the chair into the back of my vehicle. "I'm taking you for a drive. That's it."

"Pssh. I need fresh air."

"Crack a window."

He side-eyes me.

"Heard you got traded to LA," he says.

There's a full minute of silence, then I burst out laughing. "Yeah. Yeah, I did."

"We got Kyle for you. That's a good deal."

"You ever meet Kyle?"

"He's a good player."

"Who only cares about money and himself."

"What do you care about now that you've got everything you could want?"

"World peace," I say.

"Alright, Miss America."

If I had the answer, I probably wouldn't be here with no contract babysitting my geriatric former coach.

A few minutes later, I find myself pulling up in front of Kodiak Camp.

Coach hoots. "The hell are we doing here?"

"Recovering."

When I wheel Coach inside, the manager greets us each with a warm hug, then crosses to the doors and calls to some kids on the court.

"Counselors-in-training," she explains.

I go outside toward them, wheeling Coach in his chair and pulling up at the side of the asphalt. Along the horizon, there's the crest of the hill beyond which the lake looms where Nova and I went swimming. The cabins where we fooled around for the first time.

This isn't why I came here, but it calls to me. It washes over me like a wave, the longing and the freedom.

The feeling of learning there could be more to my life.

Of being seen by a pair of bright blue eyes I wanted to live in forever.

A ball hits my arm before I can grab it out of the air.

"Sorry!" one of the kids calls.

I pass it back, and he takes another shot. It bounces the same way, and I grab it again, this time crossing to give it back to him.

"Wrist," I say under my breath.

"What do you mean?"

"It's your wrist. You're involving it too early."

He snaps me the ball, and I hesitate only a second before squaring up to the basket. I haven't done this in months.

Maybe part of me thought I couldn't.

I bend my knees, rise up, and follow through. There's silence for one second. Two. The ball swishes through the net.

Hollers go up.

"Your turn." I nod to the boy, and he takes the ball, tries it. Gets it on the second go.

"I hear you need a coach," Coach calls.

The other team descends. "Hell yes."

"Hell no." I check my phone. "We gotta get back, old man."

I go to get his wheelchair, and he lifts his legs, kicking me when I get close.

I grunt. "Jesus, Coach. We'll both have bad knees after this."

"Well, stop trying to make me do what I don't want to."

My guy sulks in the corner while the other team runs circles around him with the ball.

"I'll play you for it," I decide, praying I don't regret this. "Underdogs, you're mine."

We organize the three-on-three match. It's down to the wire when the call comes in from the care home.

"He needs to be back," the employee says stubbornly.

"I know. I'm working on it."

"Can you work faster?"

"Not unless you want me to carry him out."

I click off and watch for another minute. My team sinks the final basket.

"That was solid," I tell them, clapping each player on the back.

One of the guys pants his way over to the bench, grabs a Gatorade, and drains it.

"Okay, five-on-one," one of the other guys says, pulling the guys around him and squaring off against me.

I laugh. "You guys are good, but you can't take me."

"Let's try." They look at one another, nodding. "You first, old man."

They call me the same thing I called Coach, and

my brows lift. "Now you're fucking with me." I grab the ball and dribble, running around and dunking it before snapping it back to them at half court. "You're up."

He takes it, one of the other guys screening me so he can get past and take it to the basket. The guy on the bench holds up his phone and records our game.

By the time we finish, it's dark. I'm tired in a way the workout earlier couldn't tire me out.

When I sneak Coach back into his care home, muttering every apology I know, the staff looks ready to kill me. It was worth it.

After showering, I pull up the offer from New York.

It's not objectively terrible.

I head for the second bedroom in my condo. The one time I came back since the move, I grabbed more stuff. Didn't even move out the trophies or old jerseys or photos. Rummaging through them, I find the first trophy I ever won, back when my entire life was ahead of me.

I won it at basketball camp. Like those kids today, all I wanted was to play. I was high on getting better, on feeling as though I fit in.

I click out of my email and into my texts.

Clay: I was at camp today. Thought of you. Remembering when we went swimming.

Dots appear almost instantly.

Nova: Was that all you remember?

My breath sticks in my chest.

Clay: I remember your smile.

Nova: I remember your tattoos. Your hands. The way you said my name.

I close my eyes, watch it play in my head like a movie.

Clay: That was a good day.

Nova: And today?

I turn it over.

Clay: Today was a good day too.

13

NOVA

"*O*hhhh, that's a miss." Brooke groans next to me on the couch. She slaps her controller in frustration. "Dammit, I still need practice before I can kick Jay's ass. Let's change up the teams."

Brooke wanted to hang out and get the scoop on LA, so I came over the day after I got back. She was playing *Pro Ball NOW* when I arrived, and I asked if I could try it.

It's strangely addictive.

She resets the game to the main screen, flipping through eligible players to add to her team.

"Miles know you play him?" I ask.

"Never. And you won't say a word. How's your team?"

I bite my lip and go back to the choices.

At first, I picked people I knew, including a few Kodiaks like Jay and some other big names. I steered clear of Clay because he's on my mind enough without him taking up the screen in front of me, but now I add him.

"Nice addition," Brooke comments. "You're missing a little grumpy tattooed hottie in your heart?"

"No."

"In your pants?"

I hit her on the arm and she laughs.

"He wished me luck and we talked after the show."

"And?"

"And I might have had one dream about him," I mumble.

"This dream in which you were both fully clothed and talking about the weather."

I shift down lower against the couch.

In my dream, I was still in LA the night of the premiere. After hanging up the phone, I walked to the end of the alley, and Clay was there in a dress shirt and jeans.

He backed me up against the wall and kissed me, reaching under my skirt to touch me until I was writhing against him.

"I know you miss me, Pink," he murmured against my ear. "I know you miss this."

I woke up sweaty and tangled in my sheets.

"I think he's working on himself. And I'm working on me. And right now, that's what we both need," I decide.

Still, it does strange, not unpleasant things to my insides to be playing a game with Clay's avatar.

What I appreciate most about him isn't about basketball, and it isn't only about our chemistry. I miss his quiet, growly presence. The secret smiles for me and only me.

The knock at the door has me rising to answer.

When I pull it wide, my breath sticks in my throat.

Clay's on the other side, looking gorgeous and freshly showered, his hair sticking up in every direction and his hoodie shoved up to his elbows.

"Nova." He says my name as if he's every bit as surprised as I am.

"Hey. I'm hanging with Brooke."

"I, uh..." He frowns, straightening like he needs the extra two inches in height when he's still the biggest person I've ever seen in real life. "I came to get my game back."

"We're still playing it. Come in," Brooke calls from the living room.

He ducks through the doorway and follows me inside, close enough I can smell the woodsy scent of his body wash.

Brooke shows him her team.

"Miles?" Clay scoffs.

"Watch him beat your ass," she challenges.

"My ass?" he echoes, cutting me a look. "Pink, did I make your team?"

Embarrassment rises up, warmth spreading through my cheeks.

Brooke's phone rings from the coffee table. "Yeah, I got the clothes," she answers when she picks up. "It's on my schedule for next week."

She bounces up, waving between us. *Keep playing*, she mouths.

I can't shoot my friend side-eye because she's already out of the room.

Clay sits next to me and takes Brooke's controller.

"You haven't played it in forever," I say.

He brought a small stash of games to LA, but although I'd seen him play once or twice in Denver, he never seemed to once we moved.

"Figured I might see if I remember how." He shifts next to me, lowering his body onto the couch.

It's Brooke's fault I'm suddenly hyper aware of Clay, and the fact that I haven't had an orgasm that wasn't self-perpetuated in far too long.

"You're pretty good at this," he says after we play a few sequences.

"So are you," I say as his avatar moves down the court and dunks the ball.

I throw up both hands in victory as he collapses back against the couch.

He rubs a hand over his jaw. "I'm jealous of my avatar. They haven't programmed in my knee problems yet."

I set down the controller and turn toward him,

my knee brushing his. "He's a game character. You're a real person, flesh and blood."

"You say that like it's a good thing."

My heart squeezes hard at the vulnerability in his voice.

"Tell me more about your drafting strategy," he murmurs, oblivious to the fact I'm basically undressing him in my peripheral vision.

"I pick people I like. People I think will love playing together."

He chuckles as he starts the game. "Like who?"

I rattle off my other starters. "And Jay, of course. You guys are obvious."

He swears under his breath.

"If you're honest with him about what went down, how much it sucked, I'm sure he'll forgive you," I insist.

Clay exhales. "I tried when we first went to LA. He didn't respond to my texts or my messages."

This is the first I've heard of it. The idea that Clay was too ashamed or hurt to tell me makes my chest ache. "Then try again. Things change."

"Oh yeah?" Clay hits pause on the game and turns toward me.

He shifts an elbow along the back of the couch and I jump, dropping my controller.

We both reach for it at the same time, our fingers brushing.

His knuckles are big, his hand twice the size of mine. He could easily grab two controllers in his palm, but right now, his thumb rests across the back of my hand.

"So, you and basketball. You're still taking a break?"

His dark eyes move across mine, searching. "Looks that way."

I'm aware of every nerve in my body. The ones he's lighting up with his simple touch, the ones I wish he was.

"It's only a break if it ends," I say. "Otherwise, it's just a breakup."

He leans back against the couch. "We still talking about basketball, Pink?"

My heartbeat is unsteady, as if I'm dancing instead of sitting perfectly still.

It would be so easy in this moment to say I want him back, want *us* back.

I move closer. An inch, maybe two.

My gaze drifts to his mouth and he inhales.

Clay shifts off the couch in a graceful move, straightening to tower over me. "I should go."

"What about the game?" My throat is dry.

He glances toward the PlayStation as if seeing it for the first time. "Tell Brooke she can hang on to it."

CLAY

*T*he next two days, I pick up Coach and take him to Kodiak Camp. It feels good, playing even though it's not full out.

Word gets around. The video the kid filmed the first day winds up on the internet. Soon, a bunch of Kodiak Camp staff and alum are by the court at ten in the morning when Coach and I roll up.

It's good to have the distraction from Nova.

Seeing her the other day at Brooke's, sitting next to her, touching her—all of it affected me.

I had to get the hell out of there or give in to temptation.

Not to say temptation didn't return when I was lying in bed that night.

I did what any guy trying to play it cool would do.

Listened to old voicemails and scrolled her social

media until I gave up and jerked off to the only woman I ever really loved.

These past few days, I've started to feel human again.

It's as if I'm thawing after a long-ass winter.

But she walked away. She tapped out.

All of it still hurts. Not in a butthurt, pride-scalded kind of way.

In a real, honest, wounded, "I couldn't be what she needed" kind of way.

Last time, I pressured her. Maybe that was why she followed me to LA.

I'm not making the same mistake again.

The third day, we're twenty minutes in when one of the kids is still sitting on the bench instead of playing. The camp director mentioned this kid's had a rough time lately.

I duck out and grab my water bottle, using the drink as an excuse to stand next to him.

"You sleep?" I ask.

He blinks up at me. "Nah, I'm awake."

"I meant *do* you sleep? You got that look like you don't sleep." His eyes are gray and tired, as if he's far older than his years.

"I keep thinking how I abandoned my dad," the kid says. "I'm not living with him anymore."

"Why's that?"

"He's seeing someone. It was court ordered, which is why I'm in foster care."

"How old are you?"

"Fourteen."

I rub a hand through my hair. "You know, your dad's job is to look out for you, not the other way around."

I hold out a hand, and he takes it, joining in the play.

I'm still thinking of that as we go back to drills.

The kids are especially lax on defense, letting me get to the rim for a dunk.

"That was lazy as..." I trail off as I hear a yipping sound. The next instant, a small, furry form is weaving between my legs at warp speed. "Waffles?"

He dances, panting happily, his wiggly body clad in a Kodiaks jersey.

"Slow your roll, Big Dub," a familiar voice calls.

I look over to the side of the court. *Rookie and Miles and Atlas*. It knocks the wind out of me in a way I can't blame on the court.

"What are you doing here?" I ask.

"Waffles needed to take a dump. Guess he found the perfect spot."

The dog sniffs eagerly at my shoe, and I step out of the way.

"Don't even think about it. I'll dunk you," I warn him, and he whines.

"Let's make this a real game, yeah?" Miles suggests. "Shirts and skins."

He tugs off his T-shirt and steps onto the court, and hollers go up.

I want to remind them that's not why I'm here,

but then I feel it—the hint of fires long banked inside me.

It's the first time I've felt competitive drive in months.

Miles fist-bumps me, and I drag off my T-shirt too.

"Let's go," I say, dribbling.

I remember my conversation with Nova while we played the video game. *I pick people who'll love playing together.* The earnest simplicity of it got to me.

We go two-on-two for a bit, the kids hollering. Miles and me against Rookie and Atlas. Adrenaline pounds through my veins, competitiveness giving way to sheer enjoyment.

"Can't take me," I taunt Rookie.

"Watch me. I've learned a few things in the off-season."

"Not all of us have been playing golf," Atlas says.

Back and forth, up and down the court. Passing. Weaving. Blocking. Shooting.

"You have been practicing," I say to Rookie when we all pull up and head for the side of the court, panting. "I might have to watch you play this year."

"Because the end of last year was a shit show." Rookie grabs two towels, tossing me one.

I scan the horizon, the hill next to the lake, the mountains in the distance. "Nova watched every game."

Rookie's smile fades. "No shit. Well, I'm not watching you play this year."

"Why not?"

"Because you should come back and play with us," Miles says.

I laugh. "You're joking."

But the guys only look at one another. "Nah."

It's an insane idea. Coming back.

"You too attached to LA?" Atlas asks.

I shake my head.

"The schemes don't work the same without you. Kyle's a scorer, but he doesn't watch where the rest of us are," Miles says, and Atlas nods.

"You space the floor. You see gaps in offense as well as the defense."

Okay, so my ego doesn't hate this.

"The coaching staff will come up with schemes. Harlan will fill gaps," I tell them.

"Yeah, right. There's only so much they can do," Atlas says.

"Let's play for it," Rookie decides. "One-on-one. First to ten. We win, you come back."

It's insane. There's no way to enforce it, but it's for pride.

I shove a hand through my hair, tugging on the ends. "First to ten."

Hollers go up from the crowd watching, and we take our positions.

The past few days, I've been playing around, but it's been safe. Now, there are stakes.

We go at it. Hard.

Rookie is good, better since I saw him last, but I push back.

Basket his way.

Another mine.

Back and forth, one apiece.

I have the chance to take the winning shot. I take it, and it bounces off the rim. Rookie grabs it and takes it the other way. I'm a step slow but sprint after him, pulling up to watch as he lobs it toward the hoop...

Swish.

Not a peep from a single kid or any of my former teammates. Even Coach is quiet in his chair.

"That's ten," Rookie says quietly.

Reality sinks in. I lost.

There's nothing enforceable about this. Except everyone here has it on camera, and more than the league's rules, I have my own standards.

And that matters.

Even when nothing else does.

"I'd need a contract," I hear myself say.

Miles nods. "You better get talking to Harlan."

Fuck. Am I really doing this?

I guess I am.

15

NOVA

*T*here's nothing like the feeling of losing yourself to your passion.

Since the premiere, I've started a few pieces but haven't finished anything new. I get nearly done, then can't bring myself to complete it, as if it can't be bad if I haven't declared it finished.

Even though Annie said she loved the pieces, I can't drown out the tiny voice that says I let her down in some vague way.

An unknown number pops up on my call display while I'm painting in the garage. Harlan and Mari offered to give me a room inside, but I like having a separate space from the rest of the house.

I turn my music off to answer. "Hello?"

"Nova."

"Yes?" The voice is familiar, but I can't place it.

"This is Raegan Madani. Little Queen," she goes

on, like I don't know exactly who she is. "Annie gave me your number."

"Great," is all I can say through the surprise.

"I'm playing a club in Denver next week, and I thought you could help me out. I want a mural for behind the stage. A smaller version of what you did for the Kodiaks. But I'm on a timeline."

Little Queen is a huge deal, and the fact that she remembered me and reached out personally blows my mind. It would be good to have more money coming in. Plus, it's great exposure.

"Can I get back to you?"

"By the end of the day."

After I click off, I survey the garage.

At the premiere, it sucked to have people disparaging my work in front of me.

Can I handle taking another chance?

The door to the house opens, and Mari steps into the garage.

"Hey. Have you seen my winter coat?" She frowns and crosses to a stack of Rubbermaid bins in one corner of the huge garage.

"You stuffed your coat in there?" I say, disbelieving.

"Last year, I was so happy for winter to be done I never wanted to see it again," she admits. "What's new with you?"

"Well... I just got a call from this big music producer to do a piece for her upcoming show."

"Wow." Mari blinks.

"I don't know if I should do it. It's last minute, but I want to make sure she's happy with it."

"If it's last minute, it sounds like you'd be doing her a favor," Mari points out.

"You're right. It's just hard to put myself out there again."

My sister's smile fades.

"You know, I came downstairs and saw Harlan watching this." She holds out her phone.

On it is a video of some guys playing ball on a familiar background.

It takes me a minute to realize it's one of the courts at Kodiak Camp.

And one of the guys playing is Clay.

My chest tightens as I watch him weave through the bodies for the basket, going in for a layup.

A minute later, there's a finger roll.

As he jogs back, I catch a smile on his face while Miles fist-bumps him.

He's playing for the first time in months.

"This is good, isn't it?" Mari says softly, and I blink up at her as I pass the phone back.

"It's good."

He's getting his mojo back. Maybe I need a little of that, too.

My sister rips the lid off the bin and rifles through it. "Ahah! Got you." She lifts a parka in one triumphant hand.

She heads back to the house, pausing on the

landing to glance around. "It's going to get cold in here before long. You should come inside to work."

But I'm already typing out a text to Raegan Madani.

The club is throbbing, the music pulsing through my shoes.

"You could've warned me you were going to do this!" Brooke hollers, wrapping both arms around me.

"Got to keep some surprises in life," I call back as I toss my head back and forth.

Earlier today, I got in a hair appointment to have my faded blonde dyed neon pink.

It gave me renewed optimism and energy, even before Brooke and I wound up three drinks in at the club.

At the DJ booth, Little Queen spins.

My art forms the backdrop: three abstract panels with swirling gold florals. It felt liberating to create them, and I'm so proud of myself for doing it.

Now, she flips both middle fingers toward one of the VIP booths. Some businessmen in dark suits fill the booth, one standing head and shoulders above the rest.

Brooke laughs. "Is that Harrison King? I thought they were married."

He lifts a glass in her direction, and she stares him down.

"They are," I say biting my cheek.

"Yum. I always wondered how married couples keep it fresh."

I remember hearing in the media that between his family and business and her past, they had some pretty heavy stuff going on.

It doesn't look heavy from here.

Brooke sways along with me. She's dressed in a short black jumper and sky-high heels. Her eyes sparkle. Her maroon lipstick and the braids swinging down her back give her a chic vamp vibe.

I lift the camera and tilt it down toward me, adjusting my silver halter top to push my boobs up and together for maximum cleavage and fluffing my newly-dyed hair.

Click.

"You're hot. There are any number of guys who would love to hook up with you," Brooke points out. "You've been on a break so long. Don't you think you should stop waiting?"

I glance down at my phone.

Nova: Saw you playing ball at Kodiak Camp. How'd it feel?

Grumpy Baller: Like I'm rusty as hell :)

We've been texting the past week since I got back from LA.

It feels good to talk to him. Right, even, as if my world was never fully on its axis when we weren't updating each other on our days and teasing back and forth.

Brooke lifts the phone from my fingers and I grab for it, but she holds it away. "What's the problem?" she shouts over the music.

I huff out a breath. "The problem is I'm still in it with him," I holler back.

Since the other day, all I can think about is Clay. He's still the only person I want to share every high with, every low. The one whose smile I miss at the end of a long day.

I've watched the video of him playing at Kodiak Camp a dozen times. My reaction is more than the teasing I've shared with Clay.

Arousal wraps around me like a silken rope twisting me in its grasp.

He looks good, and I know exactly how good it feels to have every inch of that body on mine.

Brooke holds out my phone with a half smile. "Then why're you here with me? A girl's got to get hers somewhere."

I take it back, staring at the text conversation with Clay.

As if I'm conjuring him from thin air, a message comes through.

Grumpy Baller: Where are you tonight? Playing my avatar again?

Nova: You wish

I click to the picture Brooke and I took, the sexy one. On impulse, I attach it to a text message, and before I lose my nerve, I hit Send.

Here's to putting yourself out there.

We keep dancing, and I'm starting to wonder if that was a dumb idea when the response comes back.

Grumpy Baller: Can't blame me

Heat strokes through me.
I'm definitely flirting with Clay.
And he's flirting with me.

Grumpy Baller: I miss it

Nova: Basketball or being with me?

Grumpy Baller: Yes

Well, damn.

"So, I have to show you something." Brooke wraps an arm around my neck. "On a break or not, you can't let this hotness go to waste."

She leads me across the room toward the bar, where I look up and my smile melts away.

Miles.

Rookie.

Clay.

It's a row of massive, attractive men with my favorite in the center.

I could back away, or I could take Brooke's advice and ride this wave of anticipation.

I wedge myself between two of them. I step on the low railing around the base of the bar and boost myself up so my ass is perched on the edge.

"Hello, boys. Miles. Rookie." My voice is drowned out by the music, but they get the idea.

"I'm not a rookie anymore."

"What do they call you?"

"Rookie," chorus Miles and Clay.

I grin and Rookie shrugs.

"You'll earn a name," Miles offers. "When we say so."

I'm above Clay's eye level, and it's a total trip. He's wearing a black shirt, sleeves rolled up to his elbows and open at the collar, revealing so much tantalizing muscle and skin and ink.

His gaze runs over me from my lips down to my toes in a line so hot I feel like checking for burns.

Behind me, women are hollering and guys are pointing at the Kodiaks.

The bartender taps me on the back, motioning urgently at me to get off the bar.

Clay's hands find my hips, and he leans over my lap to talk to the bartender. "She's fine where she is."

The guy backs off.

"Nice hair," Clay says when he straightens. His hand hasn't moved from my hip.

"Thanks." I twist a piece in my fingers. "Heard you've been playing ball."

"He's rough around the edges but it'll come back," Miles says.

Clay cuts him off with a warning look.

"What are you doing here?" I call.

"I felt like going out but should've stayed in. Some chick is texting me pics."

I cross my legs, and my skirt rides up. "Damned Kodashians. She president of your fan club or something?"

Clay does a slow sweep of my body. "I'm president of hers."

The buzz in my system is arousal—and him.

No one ever made me feel like I matter just for existing.

I reach for his arms to pull him closer, my fingers digging into the muscles as if I can leave my own marks under the swirls of ink. "I'm glad you're here." It's half shout, half murmur near his ear.

Clay's face angles toward mine. "How glad?"

It's a dare, and a tease.

The music pulses through the counter, a mass of bodies writhing in the background, all of it saying to live for today. Not worry about tomorrow.

I lean forward and grab the back of his neck, pulling him toward me.

There's no way of saying whether my lips find his first or his find mine. I don't even care. I kiss him as if we're the only people in the room.

The only people on the *planet*.

He's hot and hard and so familiar that some part of me deep down throbs in recognition.

He tastes like an addiction I swore I'd kicked but now I can't imagine going without.

"Shit," I blurt as I tear my mouth away.

I slide off the counter and across the room, tripping down the hall to one of the bathrooms.

I tug the door after me and brace myself over the sink, starting at my reflection.

I'm sweaty and wide-eyed.

What am I doing?

We're supposed to be on a break.

One we both agreed to.

Even if I confessed to Brooke that I'm not ready to turn the break into a breakup, things are way too messy.

I'm glad he's talking to the guys again and Coach and that he picked up a basketball. But has anything really changed for us?

Except here with him, caught up in the music and his closeness, seeing him with the other guys, losing myself in his smile, I couldn't resist.

I need to get hold of myself.

A banging on the door makes me jump. I open it an inch, and he's filling the space.

Clay presses inside, slamming the door and locking it behind him.

"You followed me in here? What is it with you and bathrooms?" I demand as his body crowds mine.

He ignores me. "Tell me how drunk you are."

"Not that drunk." I peer up through half-lowered lashes.

We're alone, the music pounding on the other side of the door. His attention flicks between my eyes and my mouth.

The backtracking I'm supposed to be doing evaporates from my mind.

"Nova, it's been a minute." His rasp is so low it sounds as if it's torn from his body. "If you're expecting me to shut you down, you're going to be disappointed. I'm not my best self lately."

"But you're trying." I reach up to push a piece of his hair from his face. It's softer than I remember. "Momentum is everything."

His brows pull together. "Who told you that?"

"You did."

Clay swears under his breath. It's soft, like a promise or a prayer.

That's the only thing soft about him.

He grabs my thighs and lifts me, wrapping my legs around his hips and backing me into the door. It rattles on its hinges when he slams me against the wood.

He's hard and demanding, as if it's been years since we touched and he's been counting each day.

His kisses light me up. I touch him everywhere I can reach, fumbling with the top buttons on his shirt so I can press my lips to his smooth, tattooed skin.

He shifts me onto the vanity, shoving my dress up, yanking my thong out of the way to sink two fingers inside me.

I grab onto his shoulders as my back arches to take him.

"Oh, God."

It's fast. He starts to pull back, but I grab his wrist to keep him where he is.

My head falls back against the mirror as he pumps into me, finding a rhythm.

He always chooses the rhythm.

"Look at me," he commands.

His eyes darken on mine. Sweat traces a path down my neck as my hips rock to meet him stroke for stroke.

"I'd follow you anywhere."

Clay sinks to his knees, yanking my hips to the edge of the sink and slipping his tongue between my thighs.

The music and the sweat and the tiny space and Clay's huge body overwhelm me.

My fingers twist in his hair, tugging as if I have a hope of controlling him. This.

It doesn't matter because he knows what he wants.

For the first time in months, he's here with me, completely. His body, his mind, his soul.

The blood sings in my veins as his fingers join his mouth. I can't hold back a moan, but it's loud enough outside that no one's going to hear.

My knuckles whiten on the sink behind me as I arch up into him. The pleasure from his licking, from his huge fingers curling inside me, builds until it drowns out everything else.

There's nothing to hear, or see, or smell. There's only this feeling concentrated deep in my core.

I'm a painter but he's a goddamned artist.

The pleasure and need contract until they're one throbbing point.

I'm shattering around him, against him.

He groans, his fingers digging into my skin as I ride out the feelings. I'm crashing, breaking on him like a wave on the shore.

It takes seconds or minutes for awareness to come back. Somehow he's standing. My forehead rests on his chest, the hammering of his heart echoing mine.

How did my skirt get up around my chest?

I'm reaching for it when Clay speaks.

"There's a deal on the table. No one knows. Not even my agent." I look up to see him brush a thumb across his damp mouth. "It's for one year. In Denver."

The world stops.

"Mid-market. Team's pretty good, but I left in some shitty circumstances."

I bite my lip, adrenaline seeping back into my

veins and blending with the alcohol and the arousal and the release. "Are you going to sign?"

Clay leans back against the opposite wall. His legs brush mine. "I don't know if I can take them to a win."

A match strikes deep in my chest, a tiny flickering flame sheltered between my ribs. The honesty of his statement warms me more than his presence, more than the drinks or the heat of the club.

"Then teach them how to win for themselves."

16

CLAY

"*B*allsy of you to come back," the new coach says. "You all know Clay."

"Clay who?" Rookie drawls, and the guys laugh.

I'm back at practice, and though I'm expecting there to be some bumps, I'm sure we'll be on the same page in no time. I've played with these guys, and I know how it goes.

I took the proposal to Harlan. He was surprised, but he's not stupid. The deal wasn't as good as what I'd get elsewhere, but I want to make this work. Convincing James took more effort, but I left that to Harlan—I've got zero interest in entertaining that self-centered prick.

Guess I was in a better mood than usual because of hooking up with Nova the other night at the club...

It was unplanned and sexy.

Maybe she was drunk and it meant more to me than to her.

But damn, did having my hands on her make me want to do it again.

She let me know she got home okay, but I want to talk in person not by text.

Which won't happen today because I have a pile of team stuff lined up.

"We're going to run some drills, easy to start," the coach. "Fall festival is this week, and the stadium's sold out. Let's put on a show."

The season is off to a rough start early for the Kodiaks. There are some obvious weaknesses the team has to shore up if they want to compete.

"You need to jump through a few hoops," Miles says with a grin.

I cock my head and tug on my jersey. "That so?"

"Mhmm. Doing my laundry and shit."

"How about I do this?" I grab the ball from his hands and cut past him for the basket, going up for a dunk.

The guys holler. But when I turn back, Jay's leaving the court.

"What about Jay?" Atlas says.

"You mean because he'd sooner run Clay over with his Kobes than pass to him?" Rookie says.

Looks like this is going to be harder than I thought.

I grab a Gatorade off the bench before I head in the direction Jay went.

"Where you going?" I call.

"Can't find my practice jersey," he grinds out.

I follow Jay down the hall toward the changing rooms.

"Jay—"

"I need my jersey." He stomps into the changing room and rifles through his locker. "Fucking hell."

It's strange the team doesn't have all the equipment ready.

"Here's one," I comment, reaching past him and holding up a crumpled shirt.

"I changed my number."

"When?"

"Start of the season."

That sinks in. Ours used to be reversals of one another.

He breezes past me toward the laundry room.

I stalk after him, the shirt still clutched in my hands. "Jayden. You're going to have to talk to me."

"Until when? You decide it's inconvenient?" He spins to face me, ripping the jersey out of my hand.

My nostrils flare. A confrontation was bound to happen since I rejoined the Kodiaks, but I didn't expect it to happen today.

"People leave."

"But it's how you did it." Jay slams a fist on one of the commercial dryers. "We were friends, and you didn't say shit. You got dreams? Well, so do I. We used to tell 'em to each other."

His rawness has my gut twisting.

Maybe I could've been more upfront with him about where my head was at. But letting people in, even friends I trust, has never been my default. You let people in too far, they're going to see your weaknesses.

"At the time of the trade, I didn't want to go. Before that... I thought I wanted a chance I could only get in LA. I wanted the name, the sure thing. With my knee being fucked, I needed to put everything down on one season."

"And it worked." He sighs, turning away.

"Nah, it didn't."

Jay's head snaps up.

"I got what I wanted on paper but couldn't figure out why it felt empty. I was so fucking ashamed I couldn't even talk to Nova. Ended up pushing her away. But I realized something playing at Kodiak Camp with the guys. It wasn't about the win. It's about the game.

"I think about Final Four a lot, but it's not the time on the court. It's how you and Coach were there for me. It's the guys I get to play with every day. And I want another chance to play with guys I respect. To play with Miles and Rookie and Atlas. To play with my best friend."

I reach for the jersey in his hands, tugging on it.

"That's trash," he grunts.

I ignore him and turn toward one of the washing machines.

"The fuck you doing?" he asks.

I lift the top door on the machine. The jersey goes in. He doesn't say anything but watches while I scoop soap from the commercial package. I eye the amount and dump it in.

"Shit, you washing jerseys for the entire Kodiak Camp? How dirty do you think that is?"

Jay snorts as I close the lid and read the instructions label.

Never found a use for permanent press.

Normal. Nothing normal about us.

Heavy. That seems about right.

I rotate the dial and hit the button. It starts with a satisfying rush of water.

"My rookie year, the vets made me do laundry. I fucked it up so bad they never asked again," I say.

"Smart strategy."

"I wasn't trying to be smart. I was legit that bad."

He laughs as I lean back against the machine, eyeing my friend under the fluorescent lights.

"Not a second in LA felt right," I admit. Now that the words have started to pour out, they keep coming. "I had a feeling the first time I practiced with them, but when you guys came back and Kyle..." I don't want to start shit within the team by saying how he talked about Brooke at the first game I played against the Kodiaks.

Jay eyes me, clearly wanting to believe me but still wary.

Not unlike Nova, I think suddenly. It's one thing to have a change of heart. Another to show up until you can prove it's legit, that it's going to stick.

It's going to take time to earn her trust back. And to earn Jay's.

I want to try.

"I get that these are your guys. This time, I'm coming back to help. Not to take over."

He exhales hard. "Then you gotta play with everyone. Kyle included."

"Kyles a prick."

"You're a prick."

"So, you don't want me to do your laundry all year?" I grunt.

A grinding sound comes from the washing machine, and Jay jumps.

"Don't ever touch my clothes again."

17

NOVA

"*D*ammit! I asked them to get the twelve-color palettes." Chloe waves toward the row of chairs at the table, a makeup kit set at each.

"These are great." I glance at Brooke.

"Kids should pay more for you than for me. I can barely draw a stick person," she says.

"You don't need to. You just need a basketball, a star, and a K," I remind her.

We're getting ready for Fall Fest, the team's pep-rally-style event before the Sunday home game. More importantly, it's Clay's first game back. The media lost their shit when he signed again with Denver.

Chloe was trying to come up with ideas for a kid-friendly events other than the mini-dunk contest set up at one end of the pavilion outside the stadium. I suggested face painting, and together, Brooke and I came up with a list of designs. Mari has even agreed to pass out balloons by the front gates with Emily napping in a stroller beside her.

Do I secretly want to see Clay? Sure. That could be part of it.

The Fall Festival is opening, and fans flood through the gates wearing #BEARFORCE shirts, plus a range of jerseys. I see Miles, Jay, Rookie, and of course Clay represented.

"We need to paint each other's faces first," Brooke insists as she drops onto the stool next to me. "It's advertising the product."

"What do you want?"

"A K for Kodiaks."

I start to paint a K on her smooth skin. "Be sure to tag me if you post this to social."

Brooke snorts, shaking her head until I grab her chin to make her still while I finish filling in the color.

"I'm taking the weekend off," she says.

"Everything good?" I ask, frowning.

"Just haters. When you put your life online, people feel like they get to have an opinion on every aspect of it."

"I bet it's weird having strangers expect you to behave a certain way."

"Honestly, I can ignore the random trolls who like to shout from behind a keyboard. It's the actual friends who make things hard."

I tip her face the other way and start on the opposite side. "Any friends in particular?"

She sighs. "The sorority has a big reunion event

coming up that I offered to help plan. But one of the other girls swooped in and grabbed it. Apparently, she said I would make it about me."

"Not happening. You're one of the most thoughtful, inclusive people I know." When I first came to town, Brooke was the first person to make sure I felt like part of the crew.

"She thinks I need to be the center of attention."

"Maybe you're just charismatic and the attention comes to you whether you try to grab it or not?" I hold up the mirror, and she inspects my work. The number seven.

"That's not Jay's number."

"No. You told me it was yours when you played as a kid."

Her lips curve. "You're the best, you know that? Now, I'll do you."

I sit, enjoying the sunshine as she works. We dressed in #BEARFORCE tees, mine purple with white writing and knotted around my waist. Underneath, I'm wearing cropped black tights for comfort, plus white sneakers. My hair is up in a ponytail.

"How're things going with Clay since you hooked up at the club?" Brooke asks.

My mouth falls open. "I didn't say we hooked up!"

"It was obvious from every inch of you when you came back from that bathroom. I don't need the details."

"Good."

She frowns. "I was being cool. Of course I want the details."

I glance around in case there are children within earshot. "He, ah, made a compelling case. With his…"

"His words," Brooke supplies.

"Exactly." I flush.

Since the night we hooked up, we've been texting. It started with him sending me ideas for tattoos.

Still owe you one, he reminded me.

"But?"

But I'm trying to keep my heart safe. I hope this season, being back with this team, will help him and not hurt him more.

"I need to know that we can get through the hard times. Summer was rough for both of us, and I'm not willing to go through that again. I can't."

"I get it. Following your boyfriend to LA only to have him win the championship and get injured and spiral out is the worst. But you're the one who left."

My head snaps up.

"You came to be with Mari and Emily, yes? You said you needed space. I'm not saying you shouldn't have," she goes on immediately. "A woman can leave for any reason she goddamned wants. But you acted. So, if there's something you can't handle, you need to know what that is."

I'm still turning that over when she finishes her artwork. She passes me the mirror.

146

"This better not be a purple dick..."

My mouth falls open as Clay's name and jersey number stare back at me. "Well, that's not obvious at all."

"Never hurts to plant your flag." Brooke grins.

Brooke and I turn our attention to the kids lining up for face painting, purple and black and gold balloons clutched in their hands.

For a while, we're working side by side.

Miles stops by with lemonades during a short lull in the action. "Here you go, ladies. Nice face, Nova."

"Thanks."

The crowd erupts into cheers, and we look toward the entrance.

Clay's there, surrounded by people. He's in sweatpants and a long-sleeved shirt, his Kodiaks hat on backward. But as I watch, he sheds each item, stripping down to swim trunks.

"You need a towel for that drool?" Brooke offers, and I wave her off.

"What's he doing?" I ask as I notice that he's standing next to a tank of water.

"Some charity thing. The kids wanted to dunk Coach, but he wasn't approved for that medically. So, Clay volunteered."

I watch him sit in the chair, and Kyle goes up with a ball.

"Donation first," Clay calls.

"I'd pay a lot for this." He passes a check to the attendant, then chucks the ball at the dunk spot.

It doesn't work. Clay grins.

Kyle goes up to the lever and hits it with his fist.

The crowd gasps and hollers, as many exchanging uneasy looks as laughing.

For the next few kids, I have one eye on the dunk tank and the other on my work.

"Can you take the next one?" I ask Brooke under my breath as I see Clay get out of the tank and motion that he's done for the day.

"Sure thing."

I grab a towel from my supplies and find my way over to the dunk tank.

Clay's still only wearing swim trunks, and the water drips off his perfect form.

"Hi," I say, holding out the towel.

"Hey." He grins as he takes it. The fabric is woefully insufficient for his huge body. "You look good."

His gaze settles on my cheek before coming back to my eyes.

"So do you." A flush crawls up my face as I think of the last time we were together.

My skirt up around my chest.

His tongue doing wicked things between my thighs.

"Gonna get a win, Clay?" someone calls from the crowd.

"Hell yeah."

I glance back over my shoulder, remembering

we're in public with thousands of people. "I, ah, should get back."

Before he can answer, I turn on my heel, tripping as I make my way back to the face-painting stand.

"You guys are stupid cute," Brooke says.

We're back working for a few minutes—I've finished two Ks, three jersey numbers, and a special-request purple dinosaur when a hundred-dollar bill in the jar makes me snap my eyes up.

Clay stands by my chair. It's hard to keep any distance.

"Take a seat," I offer.

Clay looks at the kid-sized chair.

"Yeah, never mind," I tell him.

I step on the chair instead, so we're eye level. He holds out a hand for the paints, and I set them in his palm. Then I go to work, outlining my design.

"I see you traded painting canvas for kids this week," he comments.

"Only for today. I'm taking over Harlan's garage. This gallery in New York that was interested in offering me a show after I did the Kodiaks mural last year had a cancellation and said they could fit me in for a solo show before Christmas."

"That's big."

"It is." I shift on my feet, excitement bubbling up. "I thought I already had most of what I'd need for the show, but the past couple of days have been super productive so now I'm going to have to pick favorites.

Harlan's going to have to sell a car just so I have room to store the canvases."

Clay turns it over. "You could rent a space."

It never occurred to me to have a dedicated space outside of a house. "That's a good idea. But..."

"I know you can afford it."

"You're right." Sometimes it still feels strange to have money in my bank account from the Kodiaks mural and the handful of jobs since. I can take care of myself and have more options than ever.

"I'll help you look, if you want. Have you thought about finding an art agent while you're at it? It sounds like you're busy enough you could use someone to field offers," he says.

I nod. "I've gotten a few inquiries, but I've been too nervous to accept them. Work is steady right now, but who's to say that will continue?"

"It'll continue, Pink. Once someone gets a taste of you, they can never get enough."

My skin tingles from his words.

He's quiet for a minute, the sounds of kids hollering and water splashing and music filling the space between us.

"You're being very patient," I observe as I work.

"Good things are worth waiting for."

I brace my hand against his skin as I paint, the simple skin-to-skin contact making my pulse scramble.

I'm painting a bear on his face. One with beautiful detail and blue eyes.

It keeps my brain occupied while I try not to lose myself in his closeness, his words.

"How does it feel to be playing again?" I ask.

"I'm trying not to expect too much from it. Just putting in the work. Trying to prove it's going to be different this time around." He shifts on his feet. "I also scheduled an appointment with my therapist."

I inhale sharply. "That's great! I know talking to Kat's helped, but—"

"How'd you know I talked to Kat about basketball?"

Caught out, I go back to my palette for more color. "Um. Because you're siblings. You talk."

"You told her to check on me after you left," he accuses.

"I didn't *tell* her, I mentioned that maybe you could use company for your ring ceremony." I turn back to him, squaring my shoulders. "Just because I left doesn't mean I stopped caring about you. Or thinking about you."

His nostrils flare as the words sink in. "Guess it's hard to be mad about that."

Once I'm finished, I hold up a mirror for him. "Do you like it?"

Clay stares me down, his eyes flicking between mine and my mouth. He's huge and tattooed and gorgeous, his dark eyes laced with gold.

His jaw twitches, and I want to stroke it, but I can't move, can't do anything but stare into his eyes.

"Feel lucky today, Wade?" a fan hollers.

Clay grabs my waist with both hands, his thumbs crossing over my bare navel as his mouth descends to claim mine.

It's not like the first time we kissed.

It's better because I know him. The light and the dark, the good and the bad.

"Now I feel lucky," he murmurs when he pulls back and heads for the stadium.

18

CLAY

*M*y first game back in a Kodiaks uniform and I'm ready to light it up. We're playing against Atlanta, who has a solid squad with some young stars.

The crowd lets out a mix of boos but mostly cheers when they announce me.

I guess some of the fans figured I wanted out too.

I'm ripping off my warmup gear when our new coach taps me on the shoulder. "I took a chance playing you both to start."

"It's going to work," I tell him, hoping I'm not lying.

When Kyle dunked me earlier, I was pissed. But Nova's face was the first thing I saw when I got out of the tank. Her pink hair. Her bright eyes. Her wide smile. When I saw my number on her cheek, I wanted to drag her into the tank with me and wrap those legs around my hips and taste her, no matter who was watching.

I settled for being close to her while she painted my face. Finding out she was trying to stay close, thinking of me even when she left, answered a question I didn't know was haunting me.

It was the happiest I've felt in forever, and there's no way I could've planned it. The sun beating down, a game about to begin...

It makes me wonder how the hell I let things get so off track.

But now, I have to focus on the game. To make it work with the roster we have, I'm shifting positions slightly.

When we take the court, Kyle leans over. "You should've stayed in LA. Kept your ring and called it a day."

"You sound jealous."

"You say you're here for the guys, but we both know that's not true." He nods to Miles on the bench, who doesn't look the happiest to be there.

My jaw flexes. "We want to win, it'll take more than any one of us."

The game starts, Atlas grabbing the jump ball.

Over the next four quarters, I play, but more than that, I watch.

There are problems with this squad.

Rookie's trying to get too many touches. Miles has been off his shooting. Jay can direct traffic on the court, but can't get past the big guys. Atlas is too slow to keep up with the other centers.

Those things are fixable.

What's tougher is Kyle.

He hogs the ball. The second it's out of Jay's hands, Kyle takes it to the basket, working in isolation.

When the game wraps, we're up eight, but Kyle stares me down as he takes a final shot just to pad his stats line.

The problem is hard to resolve, but easier to diagnose.

"He's a prick," I grunt at Jay when no one can overhear.

Jay laughs. "He's you."

"What do you think?" Nova asks as she cranes her head to look around the one-room studio.

"Ceiling's too low," I gripe.

Nova cuts me a look. "It's small for you."

I glance up at the eight-foot ceiling, pressing my hand flush against the plaster.

"But it's not for me," I finish.

I told Nova I'd help her look at studio spaces to rent.

It wasn't enough to drive her. I wanted to make this an experience.

So, this morning, I picked her up, bearing coffee and a list of potential places lined up to see.

"I have a good feeling about this one," she says as she peers out the second-floor windows and down onto the street below.

"You want to grab lunch and think it over?" I offer.

"Good idea."

She starts for the door, but I block her path. "Don't move."

I head to the car to retrieve the picnic basket in the back and return with it in hand.

"What is all that?" she marvels when I start to unpack the sandwiches and drinks and desserts.

"I figured we'd have a busy day. Fuel is important."

We sit on a blanket I brought to cover the floor. We eat and talk, and it feels good to see her smile.

"Thank you," she says as she reaches for one of the bakery cookies packed for dessert. "It was really thoughtful of you to take the whole morning off for me."

"My pleasure. And I do have an appointment this afternoon before practice." I hesitate. "It's therapy."

Her brows shoot up as she finishes her bite of cookie. "I don't know what you're going to talk about, and you don't have to tell me, but I hope it helps."

I try to put into words some of the dark thoughts that have circled my mind for months. "I've spent so long trying to be the best. I craved competition and was willing to throw everything away to win. But in doing that, I ignored the other parts of me, the parts that made me feel weak. I can't ignore them anymore."

She nods slowly. "I've been going over what happened in LA. I left you when you were at your lowest. I'm sorry."

Surprise has me frowning. "You did the right thing. I never want to make you feel bad. Or feel bad about feeling good."

She holds my gaze, and I'm encouraged by the trust on her face.

"Once you said you'd always bet on me. Well, I'll always bet on you." She finishes her cookie and shifts back on her palms.

"This is the one," she decides, looking around from her seated position.

"In that case..."

I go for the second basket, containing a bottle of champagne and an ice bucket.

She laughs in delight as I pop the cork. "It's like that show where they buy wedding dresses and drink champagne when they say yes."

"I figured we'd be celebrating if you found the studio." I pour into two glasses and hand her one.

"I love champagne," Nova admits. "I don't care if it's fancy. How can you drink bubbles and not feel like celebrating?!"

I grin as I take her in. Damn, she's beautiful like this.

The truth is I'm getting tired of this break.

I want her and me and a million small celebrations just like this.

It's a future I want to believe in. One I'm willing to work for.

"Now we need to get you an agent," I murmur over my glass as she sips happily.

"Do agents screen messages?" Her smile fades a bit as she wrinkles her nose.

"Not typically. Why?"

"Someone reached out to me on social media. I think it might be Brad."

I'm instantly on guard. "Brad like your ex?"

"Yeah. I didn't respond."

Fuck, what is this, Asshole Week?

"I'll look into it."

"No." She lays a hand on my arm. "Nothing's going to happen, and Brad's not going to show his face anywhere near me, who he jilted, or the business he stole money from."

She's smiling, but I'm not even close to satisfied.

Nova turns back to the space. "This is perfect. I need to follow up with the realtor quickly. She said she had other renters interested."

I don't tell her I already put a five-thousand-dollar deposit on every place we were seeing for the realtor to hold them until Nova decided.

You are cordially invited to Kyle Banks'
Halloween Party.

Costumes mandatory.

No photos.

NOVA

I creep down the stairs from my room. When I hit a spot on the wood floor that creaks, I wince.

Harlan's in the living room watching a game. Mari is rocking Emily to sleep in the corner.

Grumpy Baller: Changed your mind?

Clay's text lights up the phone in my pocket.

I'm not hiding from Mari and Harlan this time— just the baby.

I type back.

Nova: Be there soon.

I slip on my shoes and check my reflection in the mirror before sneaking out the front door. My hair is tied up in a blond-pink ponytail, and my blue minidress flares out around my hips from a bright rainbow belt.

Clay's car is at the end of the driveway, and I'm panting as I reach for the handle.

"Tell me you didn't go down the drainpipe," he murmurs as I tumble inside.

"Almost. Emily's going through a phase. I swear a butterfly flaps its wings on the other side of the world, and this baby wakes up."

Since he helped me find the studio, we've been texting, but we've both been busy and we haven't had time together in person. Tonight, he offered me a ride, saying he was driving a few other people.

"Where's Rookie? And Jay?" I ask, realizing we're alone.

"They, ah, decided to go ahead solo."

I reach for my seatbelt. "So, no babysitting."

"You mean them or us?"

Clay's voice is light, but there's an edge under it that makes my heartbeat accelerate.

It changes things, being alone with him.

We haven't been physical since the club, and every time I see him, I want.

Damn, do I want.

He puts the car in gear and swings toward the road, pausing to check for traffic. At the same time, he does a slow sweep of my outfit, lingering on a few places.

"You're a rainbow," he says. Clay brushes a finger

next to the bright purple painted star on my cheek. "You look good."

"The face painting inspired me. What about you?"

"I don't have a costume." He pulls onto the street.

"I thought you'd say that." With a flourish, I pull out the crown I bought. "Now you're the king of the court."

He bends his head so I can set it on top. When he straightens, the crown nearly brushes the top of the car, but it doesn't matter. He's powerful and sexy.

"How's the studio space working out?" Clay asks.

"It's great. I'm finishing up pieces for the show in New York next week." I shift, crossing my legs.

"Are you going to invite me?"

"Oh God. Please don't come. I feel good about the pieces, but I'm still learning to have a thicker skin since LA. Plus, aren't you playing back-to-backs next week?"

"Technically, yeah."

"So, technically, your ass belongs to Harlan." My mouth curves.

"I bet Brooke organized a convoy of people to go." Clay's huff of breath sounds genuinely put out, and his disappointment means more to me than his words.

"I told her not to come opening night." I bite my lip. "There're going to be lots of art critics, and it's possible they'll slam my work. Gives me a day to bounce back emotionally if I need it," I say dryly.

"You won't need it. They're going to love it."

My chest squeezes.

"Any word from Brad?" Clay goes on, killing my mojo with a single name.

I shift in my seat. "Not really." Since the initial messages, I haven't responded and I've had lots of other things to focus on.

"If you give me more details, I can have someone look into it—"

"I just want to forget it." It reminds me of a time when I felt small, so I change the subject. "I'm surprised you wanted to go to Kyle's party. You're not his biggest fan."

"Everyone on the team's going. I gotta prove I can hang with them. All of them."

Clay doesn't like Kyle, but he hasn't told me exactly what bugs him. There's lots that goes on at practice and behind the scenes the public doesn't see.

Kyle's hosting tonight's Halloween party, and everyone's feeling festive. The Kodiaks have a winning record, 5-3, including winning three in a row since Clay returned.

I texted Brooke to give her our ETA, and Miles has been bugging me to ask when we're arriving.

"Wow. Kyle's renting this place?" I say as the gates to the mansion swing open.

We head up the driveway and get out, Clay handing the keys to the valet.

The house is decorated with spooky graveyard decor outside. Headstones feature the names of rival basketball players. In the lights from the house, shadows fall across Clay's handsome face. He's all in black except for the gold crown, his tattoos curling around his neck and hands.

He grabs my arm as we start up the walkway. "People are going to ask about us. We should get on the same page."

I turn to take him in, drawn toward him either by his grip or the invisible pull that always fills the air between us.

It's moments like these that I feel compelled to spill my guts, to say my heart has only ever been his.

But I'm learning to protect my heart. And his.

"I will always care about you. I want you to be happy, and I know you want that for me. I think we sometimes rely too much on each other for that happiness."

He frowns, as if that answer is unsatisfactory. He's still studying me when a screech comes from the front door. It's Brooke, dressed as sexy Little Red Riding Hood, and someone in a full bear costume. The bear takes his head off, revealing Miles.

Inside, we hang with our friends, get drinks.

Kyle's dressed as Michael Jordan. Rookie has a black wig and glittery jacket.

"Who are you?" Clay asks.

"Kyle promised we'd both go as MJ. Miles convinced me it was Michael Jackson."

Jay and Miles high five.

"You look great," I tell Rookie.

"I know. And I can dance." He grins, moonwalking across the room.

"You're supposed to tell me what big teeth I have," Miles informs Brooke.

"That's the wolf, dumbass."

It's good to see the guys having a great time together. Their job is tough and stressful, and here at a private party, they can let loose a little.

"Dance with me," Clay says against my ear.

I feel him before I see him.

He takes the crown off his head and sets it on mine, adjusting my ponytail. Then he takes my hand and tugs me after him.

Nothing compares to being held by Clay. His arms feel like they could carry the world, but right now, they're surrounding me.

He smells amazing, and I resist the temptation to bury my face in his chest.

I miss him. God, even when he's here, I miss him.

"What you said about us needing to find our own happiness first." His lips brush my temple as he speaks. "That the whole truth, Pink? There's nothing else you think about us?"

I force my chin up.

His face is dark from shadows, but I feel his eyes burning into me.

I want our closeness, want to feel his arms around me. Want to fall asleep next to him and—

"WAFFLES?!"

The dog is missing, and Clay is dragged into helping look for him.

"Where's the bathroom?" I ask Kyle.

"Upstairs, end of the hall."

I follow his directions, tripping up there and grabbing my crown as it slips. There's a bedroom and a bathroom on the other side. I use the facilities, and on the way out, I run into Kyle in the bedroom.

"This is an amazing house," I say.

"Thanks." He shrugs. "You and Wade, you a thing?"

"It's complicated."

"I've been watching you tonight. Since before tonight. Whatever he did to let you get away, I'd never let you out of my sight."

The expression on his face has my stomach tensing. My eyes dart toward the door.

"That's flattering, but I'm not interested."

Kyle steps closer. "He'll never find out."

Kyle clearly knows nothing about me or Clay if he thinks that what would keep me from sleeping with him would be Clay finding out.

I take the crown off my head, brushing my finger across the sharp points on top. "Clay is twice the man you are. If you hit on me again, I will take this crown and stab you with it. Then we'll see who's sitting out the next game."

A dog runs between his legs. I take advantage of his surprise and scoop up Waffles, dodging Kyle to go back downstairs.

I'm still breathing hard when I find Clay talking to a few of the guys.

"I'm going home," I say.

He frowns. "I'll take you."

"No." I set Waffles down and the dog scurries off. "I'll take an Uber."

I'm not in a hurry to mention what happened with Kyle. I don't need to create more problems between them.

I feel his eyes on my back the entire way out.

20

CLAY

The next two nights, we play in Dallas.

Miles pulled a muscle and can't start, but I play my best game since I came back, shooting lights-out, grabbing passes from Jay, finding Rookie in the corner for threes, hooking up Atlas.

But Kyle's in a shitty mood and not talking about it.

He fouls up and down the court.

It's a tight loss, Kyle getting called out on fouls a few minutes before the end.

When we pile onto Bear Force One to head back, Miles and Atlas are arguing.

"What is this, self-help?" Miles taunts, trying to take the thick book open in Atlas's lap.

"Get your hand out of my bearspace," Atlas shoves at Miles. "Worry about your own game."

Rookie drops into the seat next to me.

"What's eating you?" he prompts.

"Nothing." I fuss with my headphones.

"Yeah, that's a real 'nothing' face."

I shoot him a look. "Nova. She practically ran out of the party on the weekend."

Maybe I came on too strong. I wanted to get closer to her, and instead I pushed her away.

She texted me to let me know she got home okay but hasn't been in touch since.

I know she's heading to New York for her show this week and we're getting ready for a stretch of home games.

But I can't let it go.

"It wasn't you," Rookie says.

"What do you mean?"

"When I was looking for Waffles, I found her upstairs talking with Kyle." He hesitates, glancing across the plane to the man in question. "Didn't get the background, but she didn't sound happy."

Kyle locks gazes with us, narrowing his eyes.

He's selfish, and I hate the thought of him being around her.

I have to figure this out.

Before it gets out of hand.

21

NOVA

"*A*re you ready to come out?" the gallery owner asks, teasing. She's a few years older than me and seems to understand the nerves.

I'm hiding in the back room, chewing on my cheek and pacing the storage room filled with canvases.

My first dedicated art exhibition is at a gallery in NoHo.

Brooke texted a little while ago to wish me luck and say she'd be first in line tomorrow.

The team is on a back-to-backs, so they'll be spending every second from the end of tonight's game until tomorrow's afternoon one in recovery.

My collection tonight is not about sports but people captured in motion. I like movement. It implies change, momentum, celebration. Everything changes. Everyone does.

"And here you thought no one would come," the gallery owner says.

"They are?" My heart leaps.

"We're nearing capacity."

I follow her out to the main gallery, and my jaw hits the floor when I see a few dozen people milling around with drinks and canapés in hand.

"Let me introduce you around," she says, tugging me toward a couple talking animatedly about a painting inspired by dancers in LA.

An hour later, I've managed to consume a glass of champagne and I'm buzzing happily, but it's from the atmosphere and this place.

From the corner of my eye, I see the owner sticking red dots on the name cards of not one painting but two.

My breath catches. "What does that mean?"

"Sold. At preview." She looks around. "To him." She nods discreetly. "And them." Another couple. "If we're not careful, you might sell out tonight."

She takes another red dot sticker and places it on yet a third painting.

"Who bought that one?" I ask, spinning around.

"That was someone on the phone who bought it sight unseen from the gallery's website."

Here, I am valuable. I do matter.

"Excuse me," says a pleasant voice that has the hairs lifting on my neck.

Her gaze lifts to something over my shoulder.

"We'll pick this up later," the gallery owner murmurs to me.

I turn, and the blood drains from my face. The man standing in front of me is wearing tailored jeans and a sport jacket. He has a beard, unlike the last time I saw him, but his face is the same.

"Brad," I whisper.

"Long time, Nova."

It's like seeing a ghost.

A couple moves to pass us, and Brad smiles pleasantly at them and takes my arm, moving toward the canvases.

"What are you doing here?" I demand under my breath, aware of the environment we're in. I don't want to make a scene.

"I wanted to apologize for the way things ended."

My eyes widen. "Like how you disappeared in the middle of the night without a word? This is one of those instances you could've just texted."

He blinks, surprised by my boldness. "I had to see what you've created."

I shift toward the next painting over. "Creativity is the one thing we had in common. You got creative with the company's clients and their money. And you set me up to take the fall for it."

Brad casts an uneasy look around.

"I was trying to provide security for us. You ran at the first sign of trouble."

This man shared a home with me. Asked me to be his forever.

But my gaze runs over the strokes I put on one of the canvases. There's the old version of me in that painting and the new one. Every layer is another layer of me.

I lift my chin. "I can see things through. At least when they're worth seeing through."

"Did I hear right that you're dating some basketball player? Guys like that don't stick around."

The words are aimed at the soft spots between my ribs, but they glance off.

He can't hurt me anymore.

The realization makes me stand straighter.

"As agonizing as it was to be left overnight and face the consequences of all you did, I should thank you."

"Thank me?" Brad echoes, uneasy.

"You helped me clear everything out of my life that I didn't want and made room for what I did. Now," I lift my chin, "if you're not here for the art, I'm going to ask you to leave. I know you have that part down."

I watch him trip toward the door, stumble outside and cut across the street in front of the gallery.

I never wanted to see him again, but in a way I'm glad he came. It showed me he's only a ghost with no power. A reminder of who I used to be and how far I've come.

Before I can turn back, my gaze lands on the bench outside. My heart kicks when I see a familiar form resting on the bench holding a bouquet, half illuminated by the gallery lights.

I've never run to a door so fast in my life.

CLAY

When I got to the gallery, I started to go in but stopped short when I saw her through the glass smiling with another woman.

She was wearing a pale gold dress, her hair pinned up in a pink knot on her head with dangly earrings.

She looked like an artist.

Or a goddess.

I was never much for sitting on the bench when I could be in the middle of the action, but tonight, I wanted her to have this moment for herself.

So I sat.

"You're playing back-to-back games," Nova murmurs when she sees me.

"You had your first gallery show. I needed to be here."

She smiles, her eyes shining under the streetlights, raindrops collecting on her lashes.

Which parts of her created which parts of me? Because I wasn't this man a year ago. Didn't feel these feelings before her.

"These are for you." I hold out the daisies—the

largest bouquet I could order within walking distance of the gallery. "You always said they reminded you of home. Thought you might appreciate the reminder in the big city."

Nova takes them, her slow smile and the way she cradles them in her arms making me glad I tried three different florists to find exactly the right ones.

"Who was the guy who just left?" I ask.

She huffs out a breath. "Brad."

"Your asshole ex Brad?" I spin on my heel to see if he's still out there, ready to do some damage.

"Don't even think about it." She tugs me inside.

We walk around the gallery, Nova telling me about each piece.

She's beautiful and alive, her creations on the wall. Leaving pieces of her soul on the canvas the way I leave mine on the court.

"This never would have happened without you."

"Yeah, it would've."

"No, I mean it." Her brows pull together. "You pushed me, made me believe I could be the kind of artist to have an exhibition."

"You always saw people better than I did."

"I see other people. You saw me."

As a pro athlete, I'm used to my body hurting. Around her, parts of me that usually hurt feel better, and the ones I never noticed stretch and break.

I turn over what she said earlier. "So, your ex"—I can't bring myself to say his name—"you have much to talk about?"

Nova snorts. "He showed me the things I wanted in my life."

What the fuck? She's not seriously forgiving him.

My gut twists, hard enough I think I'll be sick on the sidewalk.

Maybe she's moved on, wants different things than I thought.

"Did you eat?" she asks.

I shake my head. "Feel like Italian?"

We finish the exhibition, and the gallery owner starts to close up. Nova thanks the owner and discusses business for a bit, then she and I head over to my favorite restaurant in the city a few blocks away.

With help from the owner, we slip into a back corner table to order drinks and dinner.

"What happened to eating healthy during the season?" she teases after I put in my request for fettucine alfredo.

"Gotta live a little."

We eat, but I'm barely tasting the food. I'm too focused on her.

The curve of her cheek.

The humor in her eyes.

The knowledge I could lean over and brush my mouth over hers.

That I'd give millions to do exactly that right this moment.

"You said the ex showed you what you wanted?" I pretend it's a casual question. It means *everything*.

The past few weeks, I've been realizing how important Nova is. She's the one who holds things together for me, who keeps me from being unhealthily obsessed with basketball. Not by pulling me away from it, but by reminding me how beautiful the rest of the world is.

"A home. A family. A place where I can do my art and explore the world."

"You want those things with him?"

She blinks. "No. He showed me what I want by giving me what I didn't."

Relief slams into me, but it's short lived.

"I didn't give you that either," I admit. "I should have been there for you. When things got hard, I shut down and shut you out. I stopped being there for you when everything you did was for me. I'm sorry. I'm still working on it, but my therapist helped me figure out some of it. I've made appointments every couple of weeks for the future." I huff out a breath. "I was in a bad spiral. Like I was living in the middle of a storm I couldn't get out of. And no matter how much was good, I couldn't see my way through."

"I keep wondering if I could've helped you more."

"No. You're not responsible for the clouds. You're my rainbow, Pink. You're the good that comes after."

Her eyes soften.

We eat our dinner, and I remember how good it feels to spend time with her. It's not even about sex but just enjoying her company, how relaxed I am when she's near.

When the waiter comes with the bill, I hand him a credit card. After I pay, we head out, walking side by side.

I'm suddenly serious. "Before I met you, I thought life was as good as it would get unless I landed a title. You turned that upside down. Made me realize how much I have to learn about life and basketball. I wasn't the best player I could be, and I sure as hell wasn't the best man. You matter more than any championship. If you give me a chance, I wanna win you back. Slow and steady. You're my endgame, Nova, and I'm going to show you what that means."

Nova's silent, her brows pinched together.

It's driving me crazy not knowing where her head's at.

If she's losing her mind being this close to me, like I am with her.

I reach for her wrist, tugging her to a stop and forcing her to look up at me.

I'm a foot taller, but she's the one weighing me. Measuring me. Evaluating whether I'm worth taking a chance on.

She peers up at me from under her lashes. "Are you going back to Denver tonight?"

I reach for the back of her neck, tugging her close enough our noses bump.

"You tell me."

22

NOVA

The second the elevator doors slide closed, he's tugging me against him.

Clay bends to brush his lips across mine, once, then again.

"I missed you," he whispers, cupping my face with his hands. The tension in his voice winds me tighter.

I circle his wrists with my fingers. "I'm right here."

The doors ding open, and I lead the way to my room and fumble for the key in my bag.

His chest is pressed to my back, like some huge bodyguard who'd protect me from the world.

The door light flashes green and Clay reaches past me to push the handle.

One step inside, we're a tangle of limbs.

I drop the daisies on the floor. We trip over them, my heels catching on the carpet.

"I will try every day to be the kind of man who's worthy of you," he murmurs against my mouth. "I don't care how long it takes."

I wrap my arms around his muscled neck. His fingers stroke beneath the straps on my dress.

Every touch is reverent.

He's more vulnerable than the man I met. I'm stronger than the woman I was.

I want him close enough he's part of me and I'm part of him. So nothing and no one can separate us. Not even one another.

The hotel suite has a huge four-poster bed, and he carries me across the carpeted floor before setting me gently on my feet.

"Turn around."

I do, and he works the zipper down on my dress. It falls off, landing in a pool at my feet. When I turn back to him, his hungry gaze runs over me from my heels to my lace panties and bra.

He groans as he lays me down on the cool sheets, my hair splaying around my head.

"I told myself I forgot how you taste."

"You have a short memory," I breathe.

Clay reaches for the buttons on his shirt, unfastening them one at a time with huge hands. His gaze never leaves mine.

I shift up onto my elbows, breathless at the sight of him. He's a god, strong and eternal, but the emotion in his eyes says he's a man. He strips off his shirt, revealing the planes and muscles that make me hot for him. The ink that tells stories so his lips don't have to.

He takes his time.

Clay starts with my lips, kissing me until they're swollen.

My throat is next, my collarbone and the tops of my breasts. It's as if he needs to reassure himself I'm real.

He tugs my bra down under my breasts, pushing them up. Then he fists one hand in my hair as he lowers himself over me. He worships me, licking and sucking one nipple before moving to the other, holding me in place.

I try to reach for him, but he pins my hands over my head. It's both gentle and feral at once.

No man has ever touched me like this.

When his hand slides down my stomach under the lace of my panties, I arch against his touch.

"So beautiful," he murmurs, brushing where I'm already soaked.

He slips a finger inside me, filling me in a way that's achingly familiar. He touches me until I'm crying out around him, then he bends his mouth to me.

What feels so good is that he's here with me, body and soul.

Present.

Completely.

Every inch of intention and commitment steals

my breath. It's as if he's making up for months of questions and regrets.

If I could speak, I'd tell him he's more than accomplished it.

I reach for his pants and work them off his lean hips. He's hard and thick, arched up toward his muscled abs.

I throb.

I'm actually pulsing with want, shaking with the need to be connected with him like this.

"Clay," I whisper, and his hooded gaze finds mine. "Hurry."

"I don't want to rush this." He's still tracing a finger up the inside of my thigh. It's exploratory, teasing, as if he hasn't already touched the deepest parts of me.

"Please."

He stills for a moment.

Then he grabs me under the knees and lifts my hips up to meet him.

This first feel of his cock is dizzying. He's thick and impossibly hard.

Every time, I question whether I can take him.

More than ever, I long to try.

With a tight exhale, he shifts his hips forward.

"Oh." My fingers dig into the smooth muscle of his back. "Ohhhh," I sigh as he sinks inside inch after impossible inch.

"Goddammit, Nova. You're my heaven."

Not just heaven. *His* heaven.

I don't think I've ever wanted to be anything as much as I wanted to be his.

He rocks into me, slow strokes that takes him deeper every time.

Clay pulls back to search my face for signs of pain or distress.

He won't find any.

He could split me in two right now and I would pull him closer with white knuckles.

He thrusts. I squeeze.

I writhe. He groans.

Even as he's possessing me, I'm possessing him.

My nails rake his back, and the only word on my lips is his name.

When he comes, he cries out mine.

"Remember when you got this tattoo?" I smile as I drag my fingers along the mountain ridge on his shoulder when we're lying in bed and coming down from the high.

He nods. "One of the best nights of my life."

My brows life. "You like it that much?"

"Those were good tacos."

I hit him and he grins.

Now I'm thinking of that night too.

I bite my lip. "It must be almost time for a new one. What are you going to get? What symbolizes this year?"

"A dumpster fire?" he drawls, and I laugh.

"It's not over," I say softly.

"Thank fuck. I've got things I want to do."

Before I can ask him what things, he goes on.

"What about your tattoo? Do I get to pick it out?"

"Depends. Where would you put it?"

He runs his fingers along my arm down to my wrist. "Here."

Then he goes up to my collarbone, skimming down over the curve of my breast to rest on my ribs. "Or here." Then continuing down over my hipbone, stopping just inside. "Or maybe here."

"Oh, I see. You want what, your jersey number?"

His cock twitches against my leg. I snort in disbelief.

"I didn't say a word," Clay protests.

"No, but it turned you on. Your monster dick basically did a backflip at the thought."

His eyes crinkle.

"Promise you'll talk to me. If things get rough," I whisper. "I've gotten stronger over the last year, but I hate feeling like you're drifting and I can't help you."

"You won't."

"How do you know?"

"I know because I'm going to work on me. But mostly because I know you. I see you. You're as strong as you are beautiful."

His lips bend closer and I inch toward him, but right before they brush mine, they skim across the tip of my nose instead.

"Speaking of talking...did anything happen with Kyle at the Halloween party?"

My breath catches. "Like what?"

I wish I knew where this was coming from so I could decide how much to say. It was nothing, really. In the moment, the confrontation felt like a bigger deal than it was. But it was over in a matter of seconds.

Clay lifts a dark brow. "Anything bad."

I turn it over. It's not worth causing problems between the team. They're finally getting along, and I know how much this matters to him.

"I ran into him upstairs and told him he had a nice house. Why?"

Clay's shoulder shrugs. "He's kind of a prick."

"You're kind of a prick," I tease, playing with his hair.

"People have to stop saying that," he grumbles as he slides over me.

"If I fall asleep, am I going to wake up wearing your number in Sharpie?" I murmur against his lips, resisting his attempts to seduce me again.

"Possibly."

"Then I'll never get away from you. I'll be ruined for any other guy. Or at least any other basketball player."

He flips us so I'm on top, lacing our fingers together on both hands. "Mmm. Any other player comes for you, I'll own his ass."

Clay's lips trail down my throat, and I arch against him.

"What, you're going to write your number on him too?"

He covers my laughing mouth with his, and we don't talk again for hours.

23

CLAY

ver the next few weeks, we win more than we lose.

The guys are slowly starting to trust me again—on the court and off it.

I'm trying to find time with each of the guys. Teaching Rookie to pick the moments to be patient and the ones to be aggressive. Getting Miles out of his head about his threes. Coordinating schemes with Jay to help the ball move more easily through the opposing defence. Finding Atlas the best spots to be on court so he doesn't get caught a step behind.

Kyle seems to exist only to further his own goals and doesn't care who he steps on to do it.

But I can handle it because Nova's back in my life.

I bring coffee to her when she's working in the studio. She comes to home games to cheer me on.

After, I thank her appropriately for screaming until she's hoarse by making her scream more.

She stays over a couple nights a week. It feels a bit like being kids in college, but I promised slow and steady, and that's what I'm going to deliver.

Even if I want her to move back in with me immediately, I want her to feel secure and independent and not like she has to trade her world in for mine like she did last year.

The regular therapy sessions have been helping, but the season's starting to heat up and there's a long way to go.

As a way to offer a break and some off-court time, Harlan's hosting New Year's, and the entire team is invited.

"You got everything?" I ask Nova as she rounds to the passenger door of my car outside the home decor store.

"I think so." She frowns. "I hope we have enough decorations."

"It was a joke. You bring any more, we're going to need another car."

She arches a brow at me. "I want it to be perfect. Mari's gone back to work, and she's been so busy with Emily, I promised I'd take care of things."

I take the bin from her, resting it on my hip, and wrap my other arm around her shoulders as we walk to the car.

Brooke and Chloe meet us at Harlan's, and the girls

decorate. I volunteer my services, and they seem to enjoy telling me what to do. By the time we're done, the room is covered in gold stars plus a Kodiaks banner over the door.

"Does it look okay?" Nova asks, surveying her work.

"Better than okay," Brooke insists. "Fuck those players—we're the dream team."

Nova laughs and I shake my head.

"Someone say, 'New Year's'?" A noisemaker shrills from the door, and we turn to see Miles. Waffles, wearing a little hat, scampers in.

Rookie follows, plus Jay and Chloe. Coach and his niece come too.

Within an hour, it's officially a party.

Mari comes down from tending to Emily, and she makes careful conversation with Coach. Chloe's dancing with Rookie, Jay glaring daggers over his beer.

Kyle shows, a woman under each arm. "Now we can start." He grins. "Drinks?"

Brooke shows him where to go, eyeing up his company. "It was a plus-one."

"I play basketball. I count in twos, baby."

The girls laugh, but Brooke rolls her eyes.

"Kyle's what I thought players would be like," Brooke confides when she finds me in the corner.

"He's getting more out of control every day," I answer.

"What do you mean?"

It's not like me to talk trash about my group, but Brooke is an insider. She gets it.

"He looks off the younger guys who're in a better scoring position. Skips defensive coverages altogether. Bails on tape sessions with weak-ass excuses."

"The other guys think so too?" she asks.

"The other guys think what?" Miles asks, appearing at her shoulder from nowhere.

"Kyle," I say.

"He's not the easiest. But he scores points."

He continues on his way, but Brooke lingers, arms folded as she watches Kyle and the girls.

"I don't like the way he cornered her at his Halloween party and hit on her. She was super uncomfortable."

"Are you serious?"

Brooke's eyes widen. "You didn't know."

Rage rises up from deep in my gut.

Abandoning Brooke and her protests, I cross to Kyle, ignoring the women at his side. "You go near Nova again, you'll be out of the game longer than Coach."

"Whatever she said, it's lies. I didn't fucking touch her."

I hit him.

Kyle trips backward, reeling. Then he hits me back. I drop my shoulder and run at him, shoving him into the table, which cracks under his weight. He lands in the middle of the cake.

Nova gasps in disbelief. "What the hell is going on?"

Upstairs, the baby starts crying.

"I didn't think we'd be doing this. Especially off the court," Coach says.

I'm in the kitchen, braced against the marble island.

Kyle's in the other room, nursing a black eye with the help of his two girls.

"I can't believe you did that," Nova murmurs, holding an ice pack to my swelling knuckles. "I know you've been having trouble in games and practice, but why would you hit him?"

"Brooke told me what he said to you."

Her expression hardens. "I handled it."

"But you could've not. Why didn't you tell me?"

She swears under her breath. "Isn't it obvious? You're better than this, Clay. You hit him. At my sister's party. With her baby upstairs."

Guilt and shame creep in. "I was thinking of you."

"I need you to think of them too, because they're my family."

I exhale hard. I want to argue about this but from the expression on her face, that'll get me nowhere.

I go in search of Harlan. Instead, I find Mari in the garage, bouncing the baby.

"What are you...?"

"It's quiet," Mari says.

The guilt comes back. "That was out of line."

Her eyes widen a little.

"The table..." I hitch a thumb over my shoulder. "I'll replace it. And anything else we broke."

"You don't need—"

"I will. I'm sorry."

When I go back inside, Nova's in the kitchen alone, pacing. "Have you seen Mari?"

"Hey. She's in the garage taking a breather. I told her I fucked up and I'd make it up to her."

Her eyes widen. "You did?"

"Yeah." I'm not sure how yet, but...

Nova presses up onto her toes and kisses me. "Thank you."

Her eyes are big and wide and full of emotion.

Well, shit. Maybe there's something to humility.

"I'm not apologizing to Kyle, though."

Her hands find my biceps, her cool fingers digging into my skin. "You shouldn't hit people."

Her voice is breathier than it was a second ago.

"Oh, really?"

It might be cold outside, but the air between us is thick.

Nova nods.

"Then why are you looking at me like that, Pink?"

"I'm not looking at you like anything."

"Yeah, you are." I grin.

She bites her lip and glances over her shoulder. "My bedroom is still free. We have ten minutes before the countdown."

I toss her over my shoulder and walk her right up the stairs.

24

CLAY

"You're gonna make it," Rookie tells me. "I can feel it."

One week until all-star break, then we get real about playoffs.

Our fans are out in force, screaming from the stands.

Adrenaline pounds in my veins as I head out onto the court with the other guys.

With all-star break coming up, the coaching staff will be working on rotations for the postseason. We have a winning record, and we're sitting at six in the West. High enough to grab a spot in the first round, which has everyone buzzing.

But what no one says out loud is we're vulnerable.

Every team behind us is breathing down our necks.

Plus, we've yet to beat LA, who picked up some

starters in the off-season and is once again top in the West, or Boston, who's ruling the East. We're playing tonight's game at home, our last before a big road trip that includes both of them.

Not to mention the competition within the squad.

I want to get to the all-star game. It's unusual for a team to have multiple all-stars.

Which means it's down to Kyle and me.

The first period is strong. Miles hits his threes, and Rookie's settling into his schemes. Jay fumbles a couple passes, but I save them. Even Kyle's playing well, though I hate to admit it.

Since I hit him, he's been quieter. Probably doesn't want to get his lip split open again.

Yeah, if it'd happened on team property, I'd have lost a lot more than an apology to Harlan and Mari.

The third quarter, we're up eight.

I've got twenty already, and so does Kyle. The next play, I have a chance to pass to him in the post. I wave him off and go in for the bucket myself.

On our way back up the court, he sends me a look. "I see what you're doing," he calls.

Yeah, well, he's been doing it all year.

I can taste the win.

The next time up, Miles is open. I try to go around the defender, and he slides in front of me. The whistle shrills as I go down hard.

The entire stands erupt with protests. He's called for the foul, but my knee hurts like hell.

"You okay?" Jay asks.

"Yeah."

We're in the bonus, so I take my foul shots, then the other coach calls a time out. I walk carefully over to the bench.

"How is it?" our coach asks.

"Pretty sure I heard a pop," Kyle offers.

Motherfucker.

"There was no pop," I say.

I don't want to sit. It'll compromise my time and put Kyle more in the focus in these last few days of voting and give him an edge.

Our head trainer comes over and manipulates the joint, bending and flexing. I try not to wince.

"We should take it back and get it scanned. But it's your call if we do it now or after the game."

Kyle watches with interest. So do the other guys.

There's a hand on my shoulder. *Rookie.* "We need you, man. Not for tonight, not as an all-star next weekend. For what comes after."

Every instinct in me is to argue with the trainer, to swallow down the pain and deal with it later.

I meet Jay's gaze, and he nods. "You can fight tomorrow."

I follow our trainer back.

NOVA

Knee contusion. That's what they call it for the three games Clay sits out before the all-star break.

During the most important road trip of the year, Kyle gets named a starter.

Clay doesn't get picked as a reserve.

I saw the news pop up on my phone while I was on a lunch break from the studio.

"How's he going to be?" Brooke asks.

"I have no idea. But I'm going over tonight."

The team gave him an exemption from traveling this week since it's going to be a few days before he's back in.

I pick up donuts on the way over to his place.

When I arrive, he buzzes me in. On the table in the foyer is a mysterious black box that looks like it could hold a bowling ball.

"What's that?" I ask as I set the donuts on the table next to the box.

He looks over the back of the couch. "Agent had it shipped from LA."

"Can I see?" I bring it over to the couch where he's sitting in gray sweatpants and nothing else, watching another basketball game.

Clay pops the lock and opens the lid.

Inside is a clear glass box holding a ring the size of a watch.

Dozens, maybe hundreds, of rubies and diamonds sparkle up at us.

"Holy," I whisper.

He lifts the glass off unceremoniously and holds

out the ring. The sides are gold, studded with even more stones.

"That's your name in diamonds," I say, tracing the W-A-D-E with a finger.

"Yup. You don't have to whisper, though."

"Right." I laugh it off. "This thing is huge."

"Like I said. Good for pawning or busting drywall." His lips twitch.

"Maybe you could put it on a shelf and resist doing either. At least for the time being."

"Maybe," he agrees, his smile fading as he sets it back in the box and moves the box to the coffee table.

"How are you doing since the all-star announcement?" I ask.

"Fine. Seriously," he goes on at my expression. "It's not like last year. I'm not riding the edge. But maybe it's for the best I stay here and rehab."

"I brought you donuts, but the championship ring kind of overshadows those."

"Agree to disagree. But, I have something for you too."

He reaches for his phone on the table and types a few keys before holding it out.

On the screen is what looks like a ticket.

Scratch that—two tickets. One in his name and one in mine.

My brows pull together. "Aruba?"

"Figured we could spend the weekend there instead. We could swim. Eat pineapple. Plus, I hear sand is good for rehab."

"Pineapple," I echo.

Clay lifts me and settles me over his lap. I'm gripping the phone in one hand, his tattooed shoulder in the other.

I'm surprised and skeptical he's not more messed up over this. But it's hard to concentrate when he looks so sexy and determined.

"We should talk about this," I try once more. "The all-star thing."

He leans his head back and holds my gaze, his hands dropping. "It sucks that I wasn't chosen." *Here it comes.* "But... I've played with those guys plenty before. One more recognition doesn't have to define my career."

"Sounds like your therapist talking."

Clay lifts a shoulder. "If I'm going to pay him, it might as well rub off."

"You mean that?"

"I might have let out a couple of choice words," he admits, eyes crinkling at the corners. "But my life is more than basketball. And even though when I'm in the season all my focus is on competing, I have to hold some part of myself for everything that's not on that court. It would be fun to be normal for a change."

"Normal?" I echo, lacing my fingers around his neck.

"I hear normal people pack shorts and hats and run to the beach for a last-minute winter vacation for the vitamin D."

I'm intrigued. I can't remember the last time I did that, and I can't picture Clay having ever taken a break midseason.

"One more thing." He shifts out from under me and heads down the hall, returning a minute later with one hand behind his back and the other holding two huge purple flippers. "Remember these?"

My mouth falls open. "From your closet in LA!"

I take one from him, turning it over. "I can't believe you remembered these. They'd be perfect to take."

"Except that one would fit both your feet." He removes the other hand from behind his back. In it are two smaller pink flippers. "These ones are yours."

I'm so touched. "I love them."

"Yeah?" His grunt is hopeful.

Clay sinks back onto the couch, pulling me over his muscled body. I shift on his lap to get comfortable and am rewarded by the feel of him hardening against me.

Damn. This man is a ride I'd give my last dollar to take.

"Vitamin D, huh?" I tease.

"Mhmm." His slow grin is wicked. "You going to model those for me?"

"I didn't bring a bathing suit."

He reaches for my shirt, tugging it over my head, then skims his fingers along the underside of my breast.

"You don't need one."

25

CLAY

"This is a crock of shit." Coach's voice is raspy, but there's no hiding his disgust.

"Interesting seeing as how I had to do hundreds of hours of rehab when I fucked up my knee."

Coach sets down the light dumbbell and flips me off.

We're at the gym together, working out for both of us, but mostly it's for him.

"Body's as strong as it's going to be," he gripes when we stop for a water break.

"When you're bench pressing two-twenty, we'll talk." I reach for my own drink.

"You don't need to come with me every time," he says.

I cock my head. "Heard you don't always show up when I'm on the road."

"Todd is a dirty snitch." He glares across the

room at the forty-something head of therapy at the rehabilitation facility.

As if he hears us talking about him, Todd crosses the room, an iPad in hand. "How's it going today, Coach?"

"Fine. Was good as new weeks ago."

After months in the hospital, machines keeping him alive, he's frailer than he'd admit.

"Yes, well, it's good to continue to build strength and expand range of motion. Can you touch your toes?"

"Do I look like a goddamned ballerina?"

I cough and nod to a woman passing with a clipboard clutched in her hands.

"Am I cleared?" he asks Todd.

"For what?"

"To go back to work. The team needs me. The stand-in guy's been doing all right, but he was never head coach material."

Todd and I exchange a look. I nod to tell him I'll take this one.

"The new guy's holding shit down. Come watch practice if you don't believe me."

"Harlan doesn't want to talk about me getting my job back, but I can't sit on the sidelines forever. He likes you."

I chuckle. "Not sure that's true."

"Respects you, then. You could put in a good word," he says hopefully.

"When I get back. I'm going to Aruba for a

couple days over all-star break. Don't worry, Coach. I'll do my exercises."

"Huh. That sounds nice."

"I'd invite you, but I already got a plus-one."

He throws a towel at my head.

I'm looking forward to getting away with Nova. Yeah, it sucks to be passed over, but this is a damned good second option.

Plus, I want to show her I can handle the ups and downs of the season without going off.

Because as much as I've tried to resist it, there is a life outside basketball.

When we finish up at the gym, Coach and I head outside, and I steady him as he shifts into my car.

"What've you not done in this league?" I prompt. "Been coaching twenty years."

"Twenty-three."

"Twenty-three," I amend.

He glares at me from across the car. "You know damn well what I haven't done."

A championship.

"All the work. The late nights and early mornings and days and weeks and months on planes... you do it to win," he says wistfully.

I shrug. "You got to finals. A ring's not all that."

"Easy for you to say—you've got one."

As I pull out of the parking lot, an idea strikes me. I promised I'd take him to his favorite fast-food place after training. Once he's established at a table with his burger and fries, I pull out my phone and make a call.

"Yeah, I need it today. This afternoon." I listen, one eye on Coach devouring his burger. "I know."

More words stream through the phone.

"I'd appreciate that. Thanks."

After eating lunch, I take him to a park. He's spent months indoors, and if I'm honest, I prefer to see him in the fresh air instead of in a hospital room or a gym for rehab.

We're both bundled up in jackets, and people are skating outside on a public rink. We claim a bench nearby, watching.

"What time's practice?" he prompts.

"We're off today."

He makes a disgruntled sound, as if the idea of rest is beneath him. But when he speaks again, I wonder if he's thinking of something else entirely.

"You know why I'm here?"

"Because Todd wouldn't take you to the park."

Coach snorts. "No, I mean here *at all*. I could've tapped out during these last months. Just drifted off. God knows the doctors probably wanted me to."

"I don't think they—"

"When people talk about there being a tunnel, and a light at the end, I always thought it was bullshit. But there is a path. And there is light." He inclines his head as if he's picturing it. "But my work wasn't done."

I lean forward, my elbows on my knees. "You'll have to retire someday."

"Why? What will you do when you retire?"

I've asked myself that a lot since I got hurt but never had a satisfactory answer. "Travel with Nova and my friends. Visit my sister. Take a pottery class."

He snorts, and I laugh too.

"You're joking."

"Who the fuck knows. I'm no artist, but Nova makes it look good. Maybe I've been missing out." We sit in silence a minute before I ask, "How about you?"

"I have no idea. That's what terrifying. The not knowing."

I nod. "It's messed up, but this year signing with the Kodiaks felt like the biggest risk I've ever taken. How is it possible coming back to something you've done is more terrifying than doing something entirely new?"

"Because there are ghosts here. Ghosts of who you were. Where you've been. What you did in these halls, with these people. But after you've climbed the mountain, the most frightening thing in the world is finding yourself back at basecamp looking up."

I shift an arm across the back of the bench, watching a kid skate with who looks like his brother. The younger one falls, waits to be picked back up.

"When I was young, all I cared about was being the best," I say. "Now I look at a guy like Kyle, and I know I don't want to be that. But I don't want to keep going until my body fails more than it works. I don't want to be remembered as weak."

"You think Jordan or Kobe would've achieved what they did if they were looking for approval? They wouldn't have dared. They wouldn't have risked." Coach sniffs, tugging his toque down on his head. "We can't control how people remember us, Wade. We can only control how *we* remember us. If you go out fighting in a way you can respect, that's enough."

I'm still turning that over when a black car pulls up in the parking lot nearby. Security guards step out.

"Come on," I tell Coach, rising. "This is your ride."

We cross to the parking lot, and a guard holds the door.

I nod for Coach to get in first, and I shift into the spacious back seat after him.

Inside the limo is a huge case and another guard. The guard opens the case, and inside is the championship trophy.

Coach's eyes glass over as he inches closer, perching on the edge of the seat. His legs shake from the effort.

"The hell is that?"

"You wanted a championship," I say. "I brought you one."

The two-foot-high prize features a life-sized basketball, all of it gold. It's been held by so many legendary teams.

Coach lifts a hand, tugging off his glove as if to brush a finger over the shiny face of the trophy, but he hesitates.

His eyes tear up. "I can't."

There's a superstition around touching it if you haven't won.

I take his hand and press his palm to the mirrored surface.

"We'll do it together."

NOVA

"*I* expected you to have better stamina, Sporty Spice," Brooke calls as we head down the trail together. "Especially after three days in Aruba with Clay."

There's not enough oxygen to keep my legs pumping, not to mention for any extraneous movements.

I grin anyway. "Still recovering."

Aruba was amazing.

We swam and snorkeled, ate amazing food, posed with flamingos on a private island.

We had sex on every surface of our cabana, in the ocean, in the hot tub.

He was attentive, but more than that, we had fun.

We'd never really had a vacation before. The move to LA was abrupt, and suddenly it was our new normal.

This felt needed.

I want to take another vacation. For more than a couple of days.

"Did you let him recover?" Brooke asks.

"From the sex? Oh, you mean his knee. He thinks he'll be able to play the next game or the one after."

"You guys are almost enough to make a girl believe in love."

"We're taking it slow," I say.

I have enough income to consider getting my own place, but I want to hold off and see how things go over the next few months. My tendency is to leap into things, and I want to be more cautious for both our sakes.

But he opens up to me when he's having a rough day. He hangs out with the guys to play video games or have a drink after practice.

I've been enjoying having my own studio space. Since the gallery show, I've been experimenting with different media and subjects.

The real test will be the rest of the season, when everything is thrown outside our control. Clay's ability to play is still in question, plus all the pressure from the outside and the pressure he puts on himself.

He's a champion, inside and out.

"How's your sorority event planning going?" I ask.

"The sister who's chairing it keeps flashing her ring on Zoom calls like it's responsible for her Wi-Fi connection." She rolls her eyes. "It's as if once she got a diamond as big as her face, she'd won. This is clearly an event to show off their personal victories. Another one is fawning over her. Like all she wants in life is a successful man."

"Maybe you should introduce her to the guys on the team."

"Hell no."

"Trying to protect your sister?"

"Trying to protect the guys."

I laugh as we get to a clearing and stop to grab a drink from our packs.

My phone rings, and I reach for it. "Hey, Mar. You still good to meet for lunch tomorrow?"

"Change of plans. Work wants me to go to Paris for a month to meet with this other agency. It's really important, but I was going to say no. But then I thought that we could go together, go to the galleries we imagined as kids."

I blink in surprise. "When?"

"Next week."

"Playoffs start."

"I know. Harlan will be up in his own head. Clay will too. The best thing we can do is clear out."

I chew my lip. "Let me think about it."

I hang up and Brooke cocks her head.

"A month in Paris with your sister," she says when I finish filling her in. "Last year, you would've jumped at that."

"I know." And I do want it. I picture us pushing Emily in a stroller down beautiful streets, baskets of spring flowers everywhere. "But Clay and I are still figuring out what we can be. I don't want to risk that."

On the way back into town, Brooke and I stop by the stadium where the guys are working out in the gym.

Clay's lifting a massive barbell in a way that makes my insides go liquid.

Next to him, Miles drags off his shirt and reaches for a towel. Brooke's studying him as if she's going to be tested on it later.

The guys catch sight of us, and Clay reaches the door first.

"Hey," he murmurs with a nod.

"Hi," I say, breathless. "I'm sweaty."

"Me too." He bends to brush his lips over mine.

I don't care if he's sweaty. I'd climb Clay Wade like a jungle gym whether it's arm day or leg day.

"You should ask him about it," Brooke says.

"About what?" Clay's instantly on alert.

Dammit.

"Mari's going on this trip and she invited me." I tell him the details.

"You should go," he says.

But it's playoffs, I want to say. *I should be here.*

To make sure nothing goes wrong.

"I don't want to leave you," I say at last.

His eyes soften. "When was the last time you and Mari went away together?"

"We were supposed to when my parents died," I say.

Clay nods as though that seals it. "Then go. Bring me back some French shit."

"Fries? A beret? The *Mona Lisa*?"

"She's Italian."

I arch a brow, both impressed he knows and challenging his assertion. "She's been at the Louvre so long she's practically French."

Clay shrugs. "You get to decide where home is."

I kiss him again because I have to.

But I'm not at all sure I'm doing the right thing.

FIRST ROUND

PHOENIX

27

CLAY

"Shit," Rookie mutters as he bends over his shoe in the locker room.

I look over. "What's wrong?"

"I forgot my good luck charm. It was attached to my laces. It must have fallen off."

The playoffs are a big deal. The energy is different on the court and in the buildings.

Our first game has all the guys on edge.

Still, there's a temptation to treat the road to finals like a sprint instead of the marathon it is.

There are three rounds against other western teams, each time facing a stronger opponent. If we win the west, we go to finals against the top team in the east.

"Take a breath," I advise. "It's going to be a long forty-eight minutes if you don't."

"Or a quick one. You won't make it a shift," Kyle comments from the next locker over.

Rookie shakes his head. "Not like I practiced my entire life for this," he mutters.

"We don't need luck. We bled and sweated for this," Jay says, crossing to the center of the room from his locker opposite.

He puts his hands in the center, and I go to meet him.

"Let's get a win."

We take the floor to deafening cheers. The crowd is out in force, hollering from the time the players are announced. Chloe had shirts made up for the occasion, and those in the stands without jerseys are wearing purple #BEARFORCE playoffs shirts. The guys can tell it's a different vibe from usual.

"We're not in Kansas anymore, princess," Kyle says as he passes Rookie, grinning.

At least we have the home team advantage. Phoenix, whom we narrowly beat out for our seeding spot, is playing on our turf.

Phoenix gets the tipoff while I watch, leaning into the court every single play.

Still not thrilled I'm coming off the bench, but I'll get mine later.

Normally, I'd press my recovery hard and fast. But with Coach's advice and Nova's presence calming me down, I took it a little slower than usual.

Phoenix can't beat us with their offense. Our three-point shooting is better, thanks to Miles and Jay. But Phoenix guards hard, screens hard, plus they've got a couple of good shot-blockers to keep Atlas and Kyle at bay.

It's almost the end of the first quarter when I get in. They're on me in a second, cutting off my lanes, making me pass.

I still manage to outwit their guards for three baskets in as many minutes.

The crowd erupts. It feels right being out here. The adrenaline drowns out any doubt, any questions.

By the second quarter, they're onto me and my improvisations.

Miles is coming up dry, and Atlas is a step slow.

When I'm back on the bench, I look up into the crowd. There are thousands of faces, but none are the one I'm looking for.

Nova's not there.

Not wearing my jersey, not cheering my name.

She's in Paris with her sister.

I told her to go.

But I miss her.

She called earlier to wish me luck, plus sent a text right before warmups.

Now, with the eight-hour time difference, it's the early hours of the morning in Paris. She's probably fast asleep.

As my gut tightens, I wish she were here to give me one of those smiles that makes everything seem better. She reminds me how much I love doing this. I take a slow breath and imagine I can hear her voice. *"You should try basketball. I bet you'd be good."*

I'm in the fucking playoffs with a group of guys who deserve to be here. We aren't going down like this.

At half time, we're up four.

"Just keep one step ahead," Jay tells the guys in the locker room.

I nod. "They can rotate on us all they want, but they're going to get tired guarding that hard. Punish them when they do."

The third is evenly matched. I play half of it, winning our minutes even though my knee is twinging in protest by the end.

The start of the fourth, they pull ahead by a few. I can't breathe until we get it back to a two-point lead.

But it's too close. The clock can't run out fast enough.

"Make 'em work," I mutter as I watch Kyle dribble around.

He gets frustrated, settling for an ill-advised three that bounces off the rim and into their hands.

Phoenix takes it to the other end for two points to tie it.

"Come on," I repeat, my fists clenching at my sides.

It's as if Kyle hears me. He grabs a pass from Jay and goes hard at the basket. The defender goes up to block him, catching Kyle's leg with his own. Everyone on the bench rises in numb horror as Kyle goes down hard.

They take him off the court, the scoreboard overhead proclaiming under a minute remaining.

Tie game.

We get two free throws.

When the final buzzer sounds, our fans are ecstatic.

But it's short-lived.

We got the win, but the loss might be greater.

We sleepwalk through media, everyone thinking about Kyle.

It's an hour later when we get the update. Jay and I are still sitting in the locker room, processing what happened.

"It's a sprain. Ankle." We look up at the sound of the head trainer's voice.

Shit.

"How bad?" Jay asks.

"Too soon to say."

Kyle could be back before the end of the series or out for the year.

This is almost worse than a loss. Falling behind sucks, but with a full roster of healthy players, you have a chance.

We just lost one of our best guys.

He might be a prick, but he's an all-star.

"We'll get him back," I say with more confidence than I feel. "Keep it going."

Jay and I exchange a look.

We could lose this series.

It occurs to me for the first time.

All of this could be for nothing.

I'm a champion who came back for a victory lap. I had a chance to live forever, and instead I'll be forgotten.

NOVA

"Knock knock. Are you still asleep?" a familiar voice calls.

"What time is it?" I crack an eye without lifting my face from the pillow.

"Almost nine." Mari strides into my room with a tray and a smile.

I rub my eyes against the sun streaming in the window.

The little flat we rented is near the Eiffel Tower. We've been here for three days, and it's been beautiful. Stunning gardens, well-dressed people, and yes, pastries to die for.

"I should be making you coffee," I say groggily, pushing myself up to sitting as Mari sets the tray on my bed over my lap. "Where's Emily?"

"Playing on her mat." She nods to the other room and perches on the edge of my bed. She's already fitting into the Paris vibe in a white T-shirt and slim black pants.

I pick up the coffee and take a grateful sip.

"How late were you up?" she asks.

"Until the end of the press conferences."

Her eyes widen. "The game went until... two. I thought I did well to stay up that late."

"Four by the time the press conferences were done."

The series was two for Phoenix to two for Denver going into last night. After dropping the first game, they scrambled back to steal the next two. But the loss last night was a blow. I could sense Clay's frustration.

"What time are your meetings?" I ask.

"I don't have any today." She smiles, slow and devious. "Let's call in sick."

"Who are you and what have you done with Mari?" I demand, but it's a welcome distraction.

The three of us go to a gallery, Emily in the stroller.

"When we were kids, you never would've been caught dead in an art gallery," I comment.

She snorts as we browse together. "But I want Emily to appreciate art."

"Because successful people are well rounded and talk about everything?"

"No. Because you do."

I stare at her as we head for the exit, where someone is selling brightly colored fabric flags.

The baby wakes up, her eyes widening on them. She waves her hands, and I buy a purple one and mount it on her stroller.

We walk together, enjoying the April day.

"Why is it never this relaxing at home?" Mari sighs.

"You're always in a hurry to get places. It's easy to forget half the fun is getting there."

When we return to our flat, I send a text to Clay. It's afternoon, which means morning there.

He calls immediately.

"How was the game?" I ask.

"Tough. Kyle's been out three straight. I almost miss the prick."

"You're two and three. Another win and you're back on even ground."

"And a loss will send us out of the playoffs."

Neither of us has to say what he's thinking: that he might not have many more years of doing what he loves.

I pace out to the small living room and reach into Emily's playpen. She grabs my finger in her chubby fist.

"How's your trip?" Clay asks.

"Great. Mari and I are spending lots of time together with Emily." I smile at Emily, but my mind is on Clay. "I wish I could help."

"We need an extra fifteen points off the bench. Been working on your jump shot?"

"Dammit, knew I forgot something. You have practice?"

"Yeah, starting soon. We have to get it together for tomorrow."

"No matter what happens, you're amazing. Not

only at what you do, but at being there for your team. If I were Miles or Rookie or Jay or any of them, there's no one I'd rather be facing down this game with than you."

He's silent for a long minute, but when he speaks, his voice is rough.

"Thanks, Pink. No one's ever said anything like that to me before."

I wish he were here so I could throw my arms around him.

Instead, after we say goodbye, I flop back on my bed and stare at the ceiling.

I'm in Paris with my sister, but my heart is with Clay.

Even if I can't help him on the court, surely there's something I can do off it.

I pull out the painting stuff I brought with me and the fabric banner I bought for Emily's stroller earlier.

Mari sticks her head in. "Tomorrow I have a meeting, but I was thinking that after we could go to..." She takes in my work. "What's that?"

"Fan art for the team." I prop myself up on my elbows. "This game could mean their season, and no matter how much Clay says he can handle it, I'm worried for him. Aren't you stressed for Harlan?"

She nods slowly. "A little. But I try not to think about it because Harlan would worry about me if I was there."

It's a reminder my sister and I are different people.

"I want to be there."

Mari drops down next to me, mirroring my posture. "But aren't you having fun here? The last time you went chasing after Clay, it didn't go well."

"This time is different," I swear, hoping I'm right.

"Emily and I need you, Nova. We can't eat entire baguettes or take cute selfies ourselves."

"You don't. And maybe Clay doesn't need me either, but I want to be there for him. The past couple of weeks have been amazing, but I want to be in Denver cheering the guys on. If you're worried about childcare, I can get you an amazing babysitter, and—"

"You don't need to do that," my sister interrupts, studying me. "Go be with Clay. Emily and I will eat all the baguettes ourselves."

28

CLAY

"*T*hese fucking shoes." Atlas snaps another pair of laces. "Defective pieces of shit."

He hurls a shoe across the room, Rookie ducking in time to miss getting hit in the head.

Our big guy rarely loses his cool, but he's not the only one spinning out in his own way.

Jay's got headphones over his ears, running through what's about to happen in his mind.

Even Miles is silent, facing the lockers as he pulls on his game jersey.

There's no Kyle. He's been avoiding here since his injury.

The mood in the locker room is heavy.

This is the moment we could lose everything.

I could lose everything.

Atlas snaps another pair of laces and winds up.

I lift a hand. "You hit my head, I will take yours off."

Rookie snorts, and Atlas grunts at him.

I take a breath and think of therapy and things Nova and I talked about. What she said to me ahead of this game meant more than I could express.

I opened the journal she gave me and wrote in it for hours.

The things I want.

The ones I'm afraid of.

My gaze falls on Rookie's backpack, a torn bag from high school he insists on carrying around even now.

"I get that this series isn't what we wanted," I say, and the guys look up. "But it's a playoff series. Tell me every moment in your life, as a kid, you weren't wishing for this." I pace the room, rubbing my hands together. The tattoos on my skin twine into one another.

Jay tugs off his headphones, listening.

I pause in front of Miles. "You didn't think it'd come easy, did you?"

"This supposed to be motivating?" Rookie demands, slumping back against his locker.

I go to him next, stopping between his spread feet. "Where would you rather be? I mean it. Tell me where you'd rather be."

He closes his eyes. "I'd rather have won the championship."

"I get that you're tired. That you've already worked harder this year than you ever worked. It's not over."

Next up is Atlas.

"I'm not telling you that because I think I'm better. I'm telling you because..." I huff out a breath and rub both hands over my face. "Because I've been to the other side of the mountain... and there was nothing there."

I have their attention now.

"Two years ago, I would've told you all I wanted was the ring. I wanted to be MJ. To be Kobe. To live forever. Well, glory is cheap. Hearing your name on the wind rings hollow after a while, especially when you realize you don't even know the people saying it." I cross to Jay. "What matters is what you do. Every day. Who you do it with."

I hold out a hand.

Jay stares at it, then takes it.

"Let's make it fucking happen," he grunts.

I pull him up. He puts his hand in and motions the other guys over. One by one, they appear.

"Kodiaks on three. One, two, three, KODIAKS!"

The low holler goes up.

"Not fucking good enough," Miles bellows.

"KODIAKS!!!"

This time, it's loud enough to vibrate through the room.

My chest expands, adrenaline pumping through my veins.

We're already doing something great. I appreciate every time I get to set foot on the court with these guys. But if every guy in here pulls his weight, scrapes the bottom of his ability and effort... we have a chance at something unprecedented.

The guys are dialed in, and I am too. I will push aside every doubt in my head for this team.

Even if a piece of my heart is missing.

Security appears in the doorway and nods to me. "Someone's here to see you."

What the...? I cross to him and peer out into the hallway.

Pink hair. Bright eyes. Full lips.

Nova fills my vision like a mirage, wearing my jersey and a denim skirt, her hair down in waves around her shoulders.

"I took a commercial flight back," she says breathlessly. "I had to be here for this game. I had to see you in person, to let you know how much I love you and believe in you. Miles might make the jokes, and Rookie brings the moves, and Jay has the eyes, but you're the heart of it. This team isn't the same without you. I had to say that because watching until four in the morning in France wasn't ideal."

"You watched the last game live?"

"I watched every game live."

I didn't know how much I'd needed her until this moment. The woman who completes me. She chose us over everything.

"You make me work, Nova. I didn't make sense. I still don't, but it's better with you here." I reach a hand around her neck to pull her up to me, but she makes a noise of protest.

227

Nova pulls something out of her bag. "I told you I'd bring you something from Paris."

It's a banner painted with bears, all of my teammates' names under it.

"No Kyle?" I notice.

"He's the little one in the distance."

I kiss her hard, savoring the taste of her, the feel of her in my arms as her soft body presses against mine. She kisses me back, pressing up to wrap her arms around my back, the banner tickling my shoulders.

The guys jog out of the locker room toward the court, Miles whistling our way.

"Get off our boy, Nova! We need him for the next four quarters. After that, he's all yours."

"I didn't want to interrupt your big speech in there," she murmurs to me. I link our hands and start after the guys toward the floor, not ready to let her go. "It sounded really good."

"Oh yeah?"

She grins, both of us stopping as we reach the end of the hallway that spills out into the vast arena packed with shouting fans.

"The guys are lucky to have you. If you get tired of basketball, you could have a career in motivational speaking."

"You too. For now, I'll stick with basketball."

SECOND ROUND

HOUSTON

29

NOVA

"You got his feet? I have his head," I whisper.

"Sometimes I swear this would be easier with a live version."

Brooke and I creep down the hallway of the Four Seasons Houston with the cardboard cutout of Michael Bublé.

"When will the guys be back?" I swipe the key.

"They're still at media. We've got time."

Inside the room, we go to the bathroom. Clay's bag is on the vanity next to mine.

The mood has been decidedly giddy since Denver's first post-season series victory in years. Now, the team is on the road in Houston, and Brooke and I organized a mobile fan unit to rep the Kodiaks.

"So, you guys are rooming together again." Brooke winks at me. "Does that mean all the money you saved for an apartment is getting spent on clothes instead?"

"No! We haven't talked about moving back in together. We need to survive the season first."

Brooke starts to position the cutout in the shower. Except...

"Dammit. There's no curtain," I realize.

It's a glass door.

"We could put up towels?" she says.

"No, he'll notice those weren't up before."

"What if he thinks you had a shower?"

"I'd wait for him."

She grins. "Yeah, you would."

We're running short of time. I pull up my phone and find a livestream. Sure enough, the press conference is still going on. Reporters are interviewing Jay, who's sitting in front of a mic.

"Clay Wade had a double-double tonight, almost a triple-double with nine assists on top of thirty-two points. How much does this alleviate the team's fears about losing Kyle in the next round?"

"This is only the second series," Jay says. "There are two more rounds. But we have confidence going forward."

"Nova," Brooke starts, wary. "Is that live or recorded?"

Dammit.

Voices sound outside our room. Brooke and I scramble, setting Michael inside the bathroom door so Clay will see him the moment he comes in. Then we dive into the closet.

The door clicks, and immediately after, I hear his voice. "Yeah, it was a good—"

He's on his phone. With whom?

Brooke grabs my arm, and I grab her back in the dark.

"You still there?" Kat's voice, I realize when it comes over the speakerphone.

"Yeah." The door clicks closed and Clay moves around the room. "I'm going to let you go. Thanks for the call."

A low chuckle. "Alright. Talk soon."

Brooke and I hold our breath. Is he not going to respond to Michael?

I hear the bed creak, then rustling.

A heavy exhale.

Then a groan.

Another.

I grab the door handle and burst out. "STOP!"

Brooke's at my side.

Clay's sitting on the bed, feet extended, fully clothed and idly thumbing through a magazine. "Got you."

"Dammit!" Brooke bellows.

A knock comes at the door. I let in Jay and Miles, followed by Rookie.

"What am I missing?" Miles bursts in Kool-Aid Man-style. "Hey, Mikey B," he adds, high-fiving the cutout.

"Clay was jerking off," Brooke says, folding her arms.

"In front of both of you?" Jay frowns.

Miles grabs Brooke from behind, covering her face with both hands. "Aww, your poor virgin eyes."

She screeches, prying at his massive fingers. "Stop it, asshole!"

Chloe laughs. "We're going out to celebrate."

"Where?" I ask. "This town is not going to be pro-Denver."

"I rented us an entire club that belongs to a friend. Come on."

I start toward the door, but Clay grabs my hand.

"Meet you there in thirty," he calls out the door.

"The sight of Michael wound you up?" I murmur under my breath.

"Not Michael," he replies.

"No. Now!" Rookie says.

I bite my lip as I take in Clay. Then I turn back to the team. I smile and try for generous. "Give us fifteen."

They holler and laugh, and I shut the door.

"Fuck fifteen," Clay growls, lifting me under my legs and carrying me to the bed.

"You can't work that fast?" I murmur.

"I don't want to. I like having you in my room."

"Pretty sure it's our room."

"I'll call it anything you want as long as you're here with me." He sets me on the bed, tipping my chin up, and I spot the notebook I made for him on the nightstand.

"You still have that?"

Clay follows my line of sight and coughs. "Yeah. It helped me when you weren't here. It was like having a piece of you. When things get dark, I think about your light, and it gets me through."

I'm overwhelmed. Every cell in my body is about to burst.

Knowing I helped him get through, even in some tiny way, fills me with gratitude.

"You almost had a triple-double tonight," I say, unable to stop the smile.

"That's it, baby. Talk dirty to me." He yanks down the zipper on my dress and tugs the fabric over my head.

I shift to kneel on the bed, giving him a view of the lingerie I put on after the game as I peer up at him from under my lashes. "You went off for thirty-two."

"Fuck, I'm about to go off for more than that." He grabs the front of his shirt and rips off the buttons.

A thrill races through me as I take him in, his gorgeous body, his feral intensity.

He presses his thumb into my mouth and against my tongue as I drag down his pants. He's already huge and hard, and when I suck on him, he groans.

"Fourteen rebounds," I whisper, releasing his thumb and shifting my attention to the obvious thing between us.

Clay was a superstar tonight. He did what needed to be done for his team and millions of people.

After the game, when the door closes, I'm the one here with him.

Well, me and Michael anyway.

I wrap my hands around Clay, needing to feel him. I lick around the head of him, a bead appearing immediately at the tip. I'll never get over how insane it is that I can make him feel this way, that I'm the one he looks at as if he needs me more than air.

"Nine assists. If you'd helped out just one more time..." I tease lightly, only because he just won.

Clay grabs my chin and drags me up until our foreheads are pressed together. "Consider this the tenth."

He drops me back on the bed and spreads my legs. He's ravenous. Before long, I'm coming, my body tightening with pleasure until I'm gasping.

"That fifteen minutes?" I pant as he shifts over me.

"No." He runs a hand down my body, caressing my breast, gripping my hip.

I soak in the sight of him, his scent, the rough sound of his voice.

"You didn't check the clock," I point out.

He sinks inside me and fills me so completely I can't speak.

"Everything else will wait."

"For you?" I manage with a smile.

His eyes lock with mine. "For us."

WESTERN CONFERENCE
FINALS

LOS ANGELES

CLAY

*W*e roll up to LA riding a high, having won our first two series, doing what the oddsmakers said we couldn't.

Only now, we're staring down the barrel of the defending champions—in their building. Kyle's still out and my knee is questionable.

There's no mistaking we're underdogs as we take the court.

The first quarter is like watching a car wreck.

Atlas gets caught in the perimeter where he can't shoot or guard.

Jay gets double-teamed by bigger guards.

Miles misses his first four attempts from deep.

Rookie tries unsuccessfully to take the ball into the paint, only to get turned over by more experienced guys.

If I questioned how much trouble we'd face in LA, now I have my answer.

The Kodiaks were going in like David versus Goliath, and Goliath steamrolled us.

Forty-eight minutes of scrappy game play leave us bruised and bloodied.

In the locker room, my guys are deflated.

"If we'd had Kyle..." Rookie starts.

"Kyle doesn't give a shit," Jay replies.

"They're too good." Atlas shakes his head.

"Don't put this on them," I interrupt as I change my shoes. "You want to look at what to fix, you look at us. We *let* them do this."

I kick my locker and stalk out of the locker room to cool off.

Harlan's pacing the hall.

"You want to say something?" I call to him, and he stops.

"It was a good run. You took this team farther than we had any business going. It's been a rough couple of years, and you're showing up as professionals. You put the team ahead of yourself, and that's all I can ask."

I stare down the tunnel toward the lights.

No.

We're not giving up.

I pull out my phone and text Nova.

Clay: Do you still have that flag?

I place a call, and twenty minutes later, the entire starting lineup plus Harlan is piling into a limo.

239

"Where we going?" Rookie asks.

"It better have a drink," Atlas grumbles.

Nova and Brooke tuck in too, Waffles in Brooke's lap.

The mood is rough. When we pull up in front of our destination and pile out, the guys eye the business's sign skeptically.

I hold the door, and Nova leads the way, everyone heading inside. I shake hands with my artist.

"Was wondering when you'd be by for your next tattoo."

I hold up the flag and point at the bear in the center. "I want that."

"Where?" Jay asks.

I tug my shirt over my head, pointing to an empty spot on my chest next to my heart.

"Been saving a spot. I thought it would be for when I won the championship, but I was wrong. It was for this team. Because I've played ball a few places, but nowhere like this one. This team makes the most of what it's given. This team fights, even when it's hard. This team looks out for one another, on and off the court."

I take my seat, my gaze connecting with Nova's as the artist starts his work.

A throat clears.

Jay.

"Yeah, I want one too."

My chest expands. I hold up a fist, and Jay bumps it with his.

"And me." We both look over to see Rookie eyeing the banner.

"You mean like a little baby bear?" Miles drawls.

Rookie shoulder-checks him, and Miles only laughs.

"And me." Miles.

"I'm shocked you'd want a tattoo of something other than your own face," I say.

"Haha. There are things I love as much. Sorry, Waffles."

"Me." Atlas.

It's easy to stick together when things are going smoothly, harder when we're down and fighting back. But that's when it matters.

I'm risking my reputation and my legacy on this. And I've never felt more alive.

"Can you do it?" I ask my guy, adrenaline pounding through my veins as though we're in another game.

The tattoo artist looks around in bewilderment. "Four more?"

"Not four. Five," Harlan says, and we all turn to stare at him.

Miles beams. "Tell me you'll get it on your neck. Just, like, a big old neck tat—"

"Don't press your luck."

The artist shakes his head. "No way I can do that

many tonight. Maybe two. I suppose I can call another of my artists as a favor."

I nod my thanks as he reaches for his phone.

Hours later, we spill back onto the street. Harlan pulls me aside.

"Whatever happens, I'm proud of what you've done. We've had our problems, but I only ever wanted to see you succeed." He claps a hand on my shoulder.

I turn back to my guys, who're comparing tattoos.

"Rest up tomorrow. Then we go back in there for game two," I say. "And we play like family. They might be fast and strong, but I promise you, that's one thing LA doesn't have. We don't think about Kyle or anyone except the guys who show up in a Denver jersey to work every day. They're mercenaries. We're Kodiaks."

There's a chorus of agreement.

Harlan folds his arms, the same resolved fire sparking in his eyes. "What about you, Wade? You ready to take it to LA in your old house?"

My hands fist at my sides as the fresh ink seeps into my chest under my shirt.

"It was always a rental."

DENVER STAGES IMPRESSIVE
SECOND GAME COMEBACK
VS LA

KODIAKS TAKE TWO IN A ROW

LA PULLS EVEN TO TWO AND TWO VS DENVER IN FINALS

.

In other sports news, former Denver Kodiaks coach announces his retirement.

NOVA

Grumpy Baller: Can you come over.

*T*he game is happening later today and I'm running around when the text comes from Clay.

Alarm shoots through me.

Clay's been edgy all week, every moment he's not caught up in team practices or press conferences.

It's exciting the Kodiaks are in the position to win the conference. It would be a new record for the organization, and the entire city is buzzing.

When I get to his condo, the door's open.

I stick my head in. "Hello?" I call warily as I push the door wide.

The cool winter light filters in through the open windows, making the living room a pale gray.

Clay's Kodiak duffle sits next to the door along with his dress shoes.

He's in the kitchen leaning against the counter wearing black trousers. His hair is sticking up in every direction.

On the counter next to him is a dress shirt.

"There you are."

He lifts his head when he sees me. "Hey."

I reach for the shirt. "This will look good. They might want you to wear it. Otherwise, it'll start a riot," I tease.

When I pick it up, I spot the journal underneath.

It's open, the pages full of sloping writing.

Holy. He's been busy.

"Looks like you need a new one."

"Nah. I need you."

He pulls me between his legs and rests his forehead on mine.

"What's up?" I say, trying to keep it light.

"I just fucking want it so much," he admits.

I exhale hard. "I want it for you."

Want him to have everything he wants, everything he's worked so hard for.

"It feels different this time around," he murmurs. "In a way, it's harder."

"Because you've won before and it will feel like a disappointment if you don't?"

He frowns. "I need them to play like I know they can. Every one of them. If they do, we have a shot."

My gaze settles on the bear inked across his chest

—my design, like each of the guys got in LA. I'm never getting used to seeing that.

Clay leans in, brushing his lips over mine. He tastes like every thrill I've ever experienced, every dream I've dared to dream.

His touch is fiery, but even more, it's home.

"I love you," he murmurs. "No matter what happens today, that won't change. What you do doesn't mean shit compared to who you do it with."

I breathe him in. Every inch of this huge man bent over me.

"I love you, too," I whisper.

An alarm sounds on his phone, breaking us apart. "That must be for Coach," I guess, regretting the interruption even as I'm anticipating the day to come.

"Yeah. I told him I'd pick him up and take him to the stadium."

"I hope everything's ready for the big celebration. Did James come through?"

Since Coach announced his retirement, Chloe has been working to pull together a special acknowledgment for tonight's game.

Clay's expression darkens. "Nah. But we figured it out."

Curiosity rises up. I want to press him for more, but there's no time.

I press a kiss to his knee. "You be good. I'm watching you."

He snorts. "What makes you think you can will part of my anatomy to do your bidding, Pink?"

I cock my head, nodding toward his crotch. "Only the fact that I do it every single day."

Clay's slow grin is worth each moment of hardship we've been through.

"Okay, you have to run," I say quickly, passing him the shirt. "I'm going to use your bathroom. I'll let myself out."

"Sure. I'll see you at the game." He kisses me again, then pulls away.

"You're amazing," I call after him.

It's a relief he's approaching this in a healthy way.

I head down the hall to use the bathroom. On the way back, I glance into the sports memorabilia room and pull up short.

The glass case with his championship ring is empty.

"How's Jay feeling?" I grab Brooke's hand, willing reality to set in.

"He's a wreck." She grins. "How's Clay?"

"He tried to play it cool, but he's so not cool about this."

The stadium goes dark, and the music starts.

Spotlights with the Kodiaks logo slice through the darkness.

The announcer interrupts, "Ladies and gentlemen, tonight we have a special presentation thanking the Kodiaks' longtime former coach."

When the house lights go up, there's a video that was made for Coach's retirement. I bounce lightly on my toes, clasping my hands together as I watch. It's touching, seeing his incredible career history, watching players say how much he's meant to them. I'm in tears, and I'm not the only one.

The LA team takes the court, then Denver is announced one by one.

"What the..." Brooke starts. "What are they wearing?" she asks as she sees Atlas, then Miles bound onto the floor.

"Oh shit, Nova. Those are fierce."

Their normal playoff jerseys have been replaced with new ones: purple and gold with a gray bear in honor of Coach. The design is mine, and Harlan personally called the league to get approval for the team to wear them. Chloe worked around the clock to get the jerseys prepared.

I grin, cheering for every player. Clay is announced last, and I jump up and down, screaming until I'm hoarse.

"If the crowd could win it for them, we would," Brooke says.

The entire arena is standing from the moment Atlas takes the jump ball.

It starts out tight, back and forth.

Two points here. Two there.

Then the Kodiaks move the ball, setting Miles up for a perfect three...

And he misses.

A collective groan goes up.

The next play, Atlas trips trying to guard and they get a dunk.

Brooke grabs my hand.

By the end of the first quarter, small mistakes are adding up to a six-point deficit for the Kodiaks.

"Damn it," I whisper.

I look up at the jumbotron for a closeup of Clay as he heads back to the bench. His expression is tight as he and Jay confer.

The teams go back at it in the second.

This time, Rookie tries to take over and get his.

"Come on," I call, clapping.

Isaac, Clay's former teammate, steals the ball from him and takes it back the other way for a three.

No.

I see the moment Clay decides to make a change. His face goes from tight concern to impenetrable resolve.

He takes over in the third quarter. Puts the team on his back and carries them to even ground.

"He's playing out of his mind!" Brooke hollers. I can barely hear it over the roar of the stadium.

At the end of the third quarter, it's a tied game. Clay goes up for a dunk, and one of the LA guards goes up for the block.

"Look out!" I scream as if they can hear me. As if they're not already committed.

My heart stops as the two huge bodies fly toward one another.

Clay is focused on the basket, the other man intent on bringing him down.

They collide in mid-air.

The ball finds the hoop and cheers erupt as both players crash to the court in a pile of limbs.

Brooke and I gasp.

The other guy gets up first, but Clay doesn't move.

Denver calls a time out.

The other Kodiaks jog over to help him up. It takes far too long for him to rise, and far too much help from the other guys.

He tries to walk it off, but when his gaze finds mine, I know.

He's hurt.

"It's okay," I say under my breath. "Trust them."

Clay turns away.

"This is the worst timing." Brooke says what every person in the arena is thinking as the final seconds of the quarter expire. "They have twelve minutes to pull out something magical."

The huddle is intense, every head bowed together as the coaches and players confer.

The ref blows the whistle, and Clay stays on the bench.

But when the other Kodiaks take the floor, it's with a new energy.

Everyone chips in.

Jay grabs a steal from Isaac.

Rookie runs circles around the LA defense, cutting into the pain to get a drop-off pass from Atlas, who's moving his feet better than I've seen all season.

Miles lurks in the corners and sinks two three-pointers in the first shift.

It's working.

But LA is bringing their game up, too.

In the final two minutes, it's neck and neck. Both teams have ramped up their defences, stopping multiple attempts in a row.

At sixty seconds, it's still tied.

Thirty.

Twenty.

Ten.

LA calls a time out to draw up a play, but it's Denver that makes the first substitution.

I'm wiping a hand over my own sweating forehead when Clay rises from his seat and strips off his jacket and tearaway pants.

"What is he doing?" Brooke demands.

"He's going back out," I whisper.

He's not operating at full capacity. I can tell, and so can everyone else in here.

But they have a plan.

When the time out is over, LA inbounds the ball over Miles to Isaac, who takes off toward the basket.

Atlas is in the right place. He sets a screen that

gives Jay time to snatch the ball away from Isaac. He turns and passes to Clay, who's open near half court.

The crowd is deafening.

Clay nods to Miles, shouting something it's impossible to hear over the arena roar, and Miles takes off toward the basket.

Clay brings the ball up the court as LA scrambles to get back.

Five seconds.

He palms the ball in one hand, pulling back as he nods to Miles in the corner.

Every eye is on Clay and his intended recipient.

Four.

LA rushes to double Miles, eager to intercept the incoming pass.

Three.

Clay pivots and release the ball...

Two.

...to Rookie, slicing through the middle of the paint.

The entire arena is on its feet. We all watch, holding our breath.

With one second remaining, he rises up in front of the basket.

Every guy on the court has both eyes on the ball. Denver watches with hope, LA with horror at the deception.

Brooke grabs my hand, squeezing hard enough it hurts.

Rookie slams the ball home with both hands.

The entire building is deafening.

"They did it!" I shout.

"We did it!" Brooke hollers.

Conference champions.

We run down toward the floor to meet the guys. Even with our VIP passes, it's a few minutes before we can find our way through the confetti and security.

It helps that Clay spots us and comes to grab my hand, tugging me through the crowd.

I throw my arms in the air and he lifts me up, spinning me around. He's sweaty and triumphant and I wouldn't have him any other way.

"How does it feel?" I holler over the crowd.

"Like we fucking won." When he sets me down, he presses his grinning lips to mine.

"Please tell me your knee is okay," I murmur after pulling back an inch.

"Nothing a few days of rest won't fix," he promises.

"What happened to your championship ring from LA? The box was empty."

"I sold it to cover Coach's ceremony and chip in for his retirement. Figured it was kind of poetic."

I'm laughing and crying at once. "You did say it was only ever good for pawning or smashing drywall."

"You sold your ring?" Jay demands.

"Your championship ring?" Rookie shrieks, appalled.

Clay jerks his chin at his friends, sweat shining on his forehead.

Miles descends, wrapping a sweaty arm around each of them.

"Let's get the man a new one."

32

CLAY

Two months later

I pull up at the end of Harlan and Mari's driveway, staring down the paved path to the house.

"What're we waiting for?" Miles asks, leaning across me from the passenger seat.

"Timing is everything," Jay calls from the back.

Brooke snorts next to him. "It's a wonder you guys win a single basketball game. You'd rather sit around talking."

I shake off the nostalgia and turn up the lane. Nova comes down the steps of the house.

"What, no drainpipe?" I comment, shifting out to meet her.

"Not today." She tilts her face up, and I drop a

kiss on her lips. "Harlan and Mari say hi. Emily's not feeling great, so they're going to pass today."

"Alright. Ryan's going to meet us there. Since he bought his BMW with his new contract, he won't get in a car that isn't his."

"Ryan?"

"Rookie," Miles explains. "He sunk the shot that got us to finals. We figured it was time to call him by his name."

We both turn to look at the passenger door of my car.

Miles looks out the window, lifting his palms. "What?"

"Nova's shotgun," I say, my arm around her waist.

"So, you get what you want because you're a champion?" Miles demands.

"That's right."

"One problem." His face splits into a wide, cocky grin. "I'm a champion too."

I can't help smiling. It still sounds good six weeks after winning it all.

"Clay's a two-time champion," Brooke says from the back.

"You just want to cuddle with me."

"Oh God, don't."

But Miles is already out of the seat and rounding to the back to slide in next to Brooke.

"When was the last time you were at Red Rocks?" Nova asks under her breath as she fastens her seatbelt.

The other three are still arguing in the back.

"I think you know."

"Remind me."

I put the car in gear then thread my fingers through hers. "It was our first date."

"That was a date?!" Her blue eyes widen.

"What would you call it?"

"You sulked."

"It worked."

"Because I kissed you."

"I kissed you better." I flip her palm and press my lips to it.

Nothing as fun as rendering my girl speechless.

The guys in the back are joking about something Rookie posted on social.

"You never miss the sneaking around?" she asks me.

"Say the word and I'll steal you away and do very bad things to you just out of sight."

When we get to Red Rocks and park, Rookie's already there, getting out of his bright-purple car. "Hey, assholes."

Miles hollers, "What's wrong with your car?"

"It's a custom color."

"Looks like you ran over Barney the Dinosaur," Jay crows.

Rookie shakes him off.

"What? You give him a name and he gets touchy."

Chloe gets out of Rookie's passenger seat, and Jay's laughter dies.

Fans in Kodiaks hats wave. "You guys are amazing! Go champs."

"Can we get pics?" one of them asks.

We head over and take selfies with our fans before making our way to the VIP section.

This is the first off-season things have felt right. I'm talking with our coaching staff about my role going forward, making sure I can keep my body on track while mentoring some of the junior guys.

James got props for Coach's going-away present. I told him I wouldn't tell so long as he made a generous donation to the Kodiak Foundation.

Plus, word is the rings for this team are going to be insane. If there's one thing he can be counted on, it's buying stuff for himself.

Coach is easing into his retirement. He still coaches at Kodiak Camp and tells stories.

I still work out with him once a week to give Todd the day off.

We'll have a new rookie next year. Plus trades happening over the summer.

Including Kyle, whose contract was up. Last I heard, he hadn't yet resigned and instead got dragged to court for not paying child support.

Harlan and I talk when Nova and Mari hang out. Wouldn't say we're tight, but we understand each other. He's mellower with a kid to distract him.

"I can't believe you got us these tickets," Brooke says to Nova.

"Rae sent them over as soon as I messaged to tell her we were planning to go."

"Little Queen loves the champs!" Miles declares, flexing both arms.

Nova snorts. "We're friends."

My girl's been creating all kinds of epic art lately, and she's in demand from musicians, Hollywood, and more. I'm so fucking proud of her, but I knew she could do it the whole time.

We moved back in together this month, after the season died down, because I wanted to focus on us for a bit.

"Little Queen wouldn't answer your DMs," Brooke says.

"Bet accepted." Miles pulls out his phone and starts typing, and Brooke laughs.

We find our seats and grab drinks before the show starts.

The vibe is incredible. A wild landscape, thousands of fans. It's the best of both nature and humanity at once.

More than anything, I'm relaxed for the first time in forever. None of this would've happened if Nova hadn't come into my life. Hadn't helped me see what was real and the limitations I'd put on myself.

Midway through the show, Jay looks over and nods. I nod back.

"This what you wanted?" he asks.

"Yeah."

I grab Nova's hips and shift her in front of me, wrapping my arms around her as she sways to the music.

I'm so fucking grateful for her, every day.

I love waking up next to her, making her coffee in the morning, making her sweat at night.

Thanks to her, I know what it means to be about more than basketball. I'm not ready to retire, but when I am, I'll face it with her at my side.

I've been looking at some houses and want one with a next-level art studio for her, plus plenty of room to display her finished work. I've found something near Harlan and Mari's. Not so close we'll trip over each other, but close enough she could bike or walk over to see Emily.

For the summer, I'm planning to enjoy my girl and the downtime and my friends. I'll give her everything, and we'll do it all together.

Next year, my Kodiaks will try to run it back and win again.

We'll be defending champs this time. The bull's-eye is on our backs, and everyone—including LA and Boston—will be gunning to take us down.

As the show wraps after a couple encores and we head out, I hear noises in the dark beyond the parking lot. Howls, rustling.

Rookie jumps. "The fuck is that?"

"You scared?" Miles teases. "Maybe your purple-dino car will save you."

I scan our friends before my gaze lands on Nova. Her expression softens with shared understanding.

"They're a family. They're going to protect their own," Nova says, smiling.

I drag her against my side, tucking her under my arm as the crew of us heads toward our vehicles in the dark.

So will I.

EPILOGUE

NOVA

"*E*verything better be vegan this time," I mutter, stirring the pot on the stove.

My feet ache from breaking in new shoes for tonight, and I chewed my lipstick off my mouth hours ago.

Clay and I are hosting dinner at our new house to celebrate Emily's first birthday.

Harlan and Mari had a party for her, but this is for family.

I want tonight to be perfect. I still have memories of Mari's bachelorette party when I messed up the cupcakes.

"We made it ourselves," Chloe points out, picking up plates to set the table. Halfway across her kitchen, she pauses, eyes widening. "Except..."

"What?!" My heart leaps into my throat.

Her eyes brighten. "Kidding. Everything's

perfect. Besides, Mar's been mainlining dairy since she had Emily. Bodies are weird."

The front door opens, and there are Clay and Jay, carrying alcohol. "Got the wine."

"I love you," I exhale.

"Both of us?" Jay asks, cocking his head.

"If that bag is full of vintage alcohol, then yes."

Clay sets his bag on the counter and comes up behind me.

"Can we help?" Jay offers.

Chloe finishes washing her hands and dries them before she lifts a bottle from the bag, groaning. "Open. Pour." She hands it to Jay, who salutes.

"It smells really good in here," Jay says as he gets to work.

"You're not just saying that?"

"Nah. I always wanted..."

The guys look at each other.

"Vegan pumpkin risotto," I supply.

"Yeah, that."

When Harlan and Mari come over, they're already in the middle of a conversation, Emily's carrier in Harlan's arms.

"She hates this outfit," Mari frets.

"She'll be fine," Harlan insists. "You're a great mom, Mar, and Emily knows it." He turns a smile on us. "Nova, Clay, thank you for having us."

Clay serves drinks as Chloe and I finish preparing the meal. Harlan sets Emily's carrier next to the couch.

Chloe and I bring the food to the dining room.

"This looks amazing," Mari says once we're all seated.

"Surprised?" I ask.

"No."

Harlan covers his laugh with a cough.

The meal is delicious. The six of us eat risotto and talk about life, and work, and movies and TV as though we're all friends. I suppose we are.

"You guys are cute," I say after a glass and a half of wine, waving my fork between Chloe and Jay. "I never heard why things ended."

They exchange a look.

"It was Jay's fault," Chloe says.

"That's some bullshit," he says before she finishes.

"You look so good together," I say.

Mari catches my eye, shaking her head as if she's thinking the same. My lips twitch.

After, we do presents. Emily opens them with help from Mari.

"It's... a purple basketball!" Mari says with feigned enthusiasm when they open the package from Jay.

"Gotta start 'er soon if she's going to be pro, right Clay?"

"Hell yeah."

"They're bath paints," I explain when she opens the gift from us. "So she can make art on the side of the bathtub. It washes off, I promise."

Then, there's a cake with a sparkler. We sing for Emily, and Mari blows out the candle.

Jay shifts in his seat. "When Brooke and I were growing up, everyone got a wish for the year."

We're silent for a minute as we each do it.

"Everyone got theirs?" Jay asks.

I cut a look at Clay as I think about what I want.

We nod one by one.

"Now what?" I ask.

"Now we eat cake."

Once the meal is done, Clay ensures everyone's glasses are full.

"I ordered something special," I say, ushering everyone out to the balcony at sunset.

"What is it?" Mari asks, glancing around.

The fireworks start.

Mari gasps. "You did this?"

I nod. "They were your favorite when we were kids. You asked for them for your birthday, and our parents always said—"

"Fireworks are for holidays," she finishes. "And I said my birthday was a holiday."

"Thought we could start a tradition for Emily. You and I moved around, but we were always under the same sky."

She throws her arms around me.

I rest my head on her shoulder. "What'd you wish for, Mar?"

"That I can fit in here as well as you do."

On my other side, Clay takes my hand and

squeezes. I squeeze back and watch the lights dance across the horizon, each color blazing and shimmering and fading into the next.

"You did this."

Clay's murmur makes me turn toward him.

"I know. I got the fireworks."

"No, I mean all of this. You stuck this group together. You came looking to put your family back together, and you made a whole new one."

My eyes tear up.

"Oh! I almost forgot." I rush to the fridge for a bottle.

I'm wrestling with the cork when I hear Clay come up behind me.

"What's going on?"

"Need. The champagne. To celebrate." I blow the hair from my face.

"Allow me."

"I've got it. But thanks." I grind my teeth together as I feel him behind me. "Can't have the perfect celebration without—"

"I can't do it." His words are a groan. "I wanted to wait another night, but I can't with you looking like this."

I turn and find Clay on one knee on the tile.

One hand flies to my mouth. The other's still gripping the bottle, my thumb on the cork.

"Nova, we always seem to have these moments at Harlan and your sister's events, which is kind of fucked, but I can't wait. You've been it for me since the day you sat in my seat."

He reaches into his pocket and produces a box.

"You took a chance on me that day. You let me into your heart and showed me what it meant to have a life worth living."

Clay flips open the box, his eyes never leaving mine.

"I've been chasing a championship ring my whole career. Lately, the only ring I can think about is this one."

Inside is a ring with a pink diamond, so huge and bright it sends thousands of sparkling rainbows dancing over the cupboards and walls.

My lungs squeeze hard.

So do my hands.

The cork pops out of the bottle and hits the wall, champagne streaming out of the bottle and over my bare arms.

"You stole my heart on that godforsaken plane. I have a better life than I deserve, and I don't want any of it without you. Marry me."

"Yes," I whisper. "But it was my seat—"

Clay kisses me hard, not releasing me until everyone comes into the kitchen.

"You know what this means," Jay says, looking around. "Team honeymoon!" he declares at the same time as Chloe says, "Another pre-season wedding?!"

"No," Mari and I say at the same time.

But then Clay's kissing me again, and that's all that matters.

Thank you for reading Play Maker. Clay and Nova have etched a place in my heart, and I hope you love them as much as I do.

If you can't get enough Kodiaks, I have news: Miles' story is coming in 2024!

Hard to Fake is a steamy fake dating, best friend's brother romance you'll never forget.

To learn more and pre-order, click here.

Sign up for Piper Lawson's newsletter to get free books, exclusive deals and more.
You'll instantly receive a steamy exclusive Clay and Nova bonus scene set in Aruba!
https://bookhip.com/GQWZRAQ

Thank you for your support,

Love,

Piper

~

PSST! If you enjoyed Clay and Nova's sexy, grumpy sunshine, banter-filled age gap romance, you'll LOVE my Wicked series.

When student Haley lands an internship on rock god Jax Jamieson's tour, she doesn't plan to fall for him—or to catch his eye in return.

Read a short excerpt of Good Girl (Wicked #1) below

CHAPTER ONE
Haley

Nothing in twenty years prepares me for that man on his knees.

Naked to the waist.

Sweat gleaming on his shoulders.

The spotlight caresses the ridges of a body cut from stone as though it wants to follow him around forever.

Maybe it does.

But he's not stone. His skin would be warm, not cold.

Silhouetted hands reach for him over the edge of the stage, like something out of Dante's *Inferno*. Souls in hell grasping for their last chance at heaven. That seems misguided because the way Jax Jamieson grips a mic is straight-up sinful.

Next to the poster is a photo of four men in tuxes, gold statues in their hands.

We're attracted to gold for its sheen, its promise of something elite and revered and sacred.

My gaze drags back to the man in the poster. *Elite. Revered. Sacred.*

"I've read your resume. Now tell me why you're really qualified."

The dress pants that were a bad damn idea slip on the seat. The polyester scrapes along my skin, and I force eye contact with the woman interviewing me. "I reset at least two hundred undergrad passwords a week. And I make a lot of coffee. My roommate says I'm better than the baristas at her café."

"Excuse me?"

The printed job description sticks to my fingers. "'Technical support and other duties as appropriate.'

That's what you mean, right? Rebooting computers and making coffee?"

She holds up a hand. "Miss Telfer, Wicked Records is the only private label that has survived everything from Napster to streaming. There are two hundred applications for this internship. Our interns write and produce music. Run festivals."

The woman looks as if she missed getting tickets to the Stones' Voodoo Lounge tour and has been holding a grudge ever since.

Or maybe she was the next one into the record store behind me the day I found *Dark Side of the Moon* on vinyl in Topeka.

It's probably not a fair assessment. Under that harsh exterior, she could be genuinely kind and passionate about music.

Maybe I'm in *The Devil Wears Prada* and this woman's my Stanley Tucci.

"I run an open mic night on campus," I try. "And I'm a developer. I write code practically every day, and lot of people fork my repos on GitHub, and..." My gaze sneaks back to the poster.

"Don't get too excited," she warns. "Whoever gets this job"—her tone says it's not me—"won't work with the talent. Especially that talent."

Her final questions are nails in my coffin. Closed-ended things like if the address on my forms is right and if the transcripts I submitted are up to date.

She holds out a hand at the end, and I hold my breath.

Her skin's cold, like her heart decided not to pump blood that far.

I drop her hand as fast as I can. Then I shoulder my backpack and slink out the door.

The idea that the biggest rock star of the last ten years just saw me bomb—even if it was only his poster—is depressing.

I'm on the second bus back across Philly to campus before the full weight of disappointment hits me.

Are college juniors supposed to have run music festivals in order to pour coffee? Because I missed that memo.

I drop my backpack at our two-bedroom apartment, change out of my weird interview pants and into torn skinny jeans and my mom's brown leather jacket, then make two coffees and walk to campus, the UPenn and Hello Kitty travel mugs in tow.

"Excuse me." A girl stops me on the way into the café, right beside the sign that says *Live Music!* "There's a cover tonight."

"I'm here every week." My smile fades when I realize she really has no clue who I am. I point to my chest. "Haley. I get the bands."

"Really?" She cocks her head. "I've never noticed you."

The table at the back is de facto mine, and I set the travel mugs down before crossing to the stage.

The guy there frowns as he plays notes on his

guitar with one hand, holding the headphones attached to the soundboard. When he notices me, a grin splits his face. "Haley. You like the new board?"

"I like it if it works." I take the headphones and nod at his guitar.

The first chord he plays is like the snapping of a hypnotist's fingers. My world reduces to the vibrations and waves from Dale's guitar.

I adjust the levels on the board. "There. You should be good."

Before I can lift my head, Dale's tugging the headphones off my ears. I jerk back like I've been scalded, but he doesn't notice my jumpiness.

His earnest brown eyes are level with mine. "Perfect, Haley. Thanks, Haley." *Did he say my name twice?* "You should sing with us tonight."

I glance toward the back of the café that's starting to fill. "Ah, I don't think so. I have to..." I make a motion with my fingers, and Dale raises a brow.

"Masturbate?"

I frown. "No. Code."

"Right."

I retreat to my table. The second chair is occupied.

"He tried to touch me," I say under my breath.

My roommate Serena tosses her honey-blond hair in a move that's deceptively casual. "That asshole." I roll my eyes. "You know some people communicate affection through touch. It's even welcomed."

"In hell," I say darkly as I drop into my chair.

"We have our own bodies for a reason. I don't understand how some people think it's okay to stand super close to someone. And don't get me started on whispering." I shiver, remembering the contact. "If I wanted some random person to breathe on my face or grope me? I'd ask for it. I'd stand there waving a sign saying, 'Please God, run your unfamiliar hands all over my skin'."

"If you did that on campus, there would be a pileup." She winks before turning back to the stage, where Dale's bandmates have joined him and are getting ready to start their set. "Do you think Dale knows you have a man in your life? Because he's not getting so much as a 'maybe, if I'm drunk' unless his name is Carter."

"*Professor* Carter," I remind her. "He's twenty-eight and has a PhD from MIT."

"Whatever. He's cute in glasses. But he lost my respect when he bailed on your research assistant gig."

"He didn't bail. His funding fell through. It would've been perfect since I'd have more time to work on my program, but at least he's still supervising my senior project next year."

"That's his job." She snorts. "But I think he likes you tripping over him."

The look she shoots me has me shaking my head as I glance toward the stage.

Dale's no Jax Jamieson, but his latest is pretty

good. The band's super acoustic, and they have a modern sound that plays well with a college crowd.

"Come on," Serena presses. "He doesn't love having college girls undressing him with their teenage eyes in Comp Sci 101? Yeah right. The man might be young enough to have danced to Britney Spears at prom, but thanks to Mr. 'Oops, I Did it Again,' you have two days to find a job so you don't get kicked out of the co-op program."

I flip open the lid of my computer. "It's my fault, not his. I suck at interviews. I haven't had to get a job before." Serena's smile slides, and I wince. "Okay, stop giving me the 'sorry your mom's dead' look."

"It's not just 'sorry your mom's dead.' There's a side of 'I can't believe you have to pay your own college.'" Serena's parents are loaded and generous.

"If it wasn't for the requirement to be employed by an actual company, I could spend the summer working on my program and enter it in that competition."

When my mom died last year, I took a semester off, lost my scholarships, and missed the financial aid deadline. Now I have to come up with tuition myself. I know I can figure it out because a lot of people do it, but if I win the coding competition in July, that'll help big time.

"Where were you interviewing today?"

I blow out a breath. "Wicked."

She shifts forward, her eyes brightening. "Shit. Did you see him?"

I don't have to ask who she means. A low-grade hum buzzes through me that has nothing to do with the music in the background.

"Jax Jamieson doesn't hang around the studio like a potted fern," I point out. "He's on tour."

"I don't care what kind of nerd god Carter is. Jax Jamieson is way better with his hands, and his mouth. Any girl would love having that mouth whisper dirty secrets in her ear. Even you."

I shift back in my seat, propping my Converse sneakers on the opposite chair across and fingering the edge of my jacket.

"I don't need to get laid. I've been there." I take a sip of coffee, and my brain lights up even before I swallow. "The travel agent promised Hawaii. Instead it was Siberia."

"Cold, numbing, and character building?"

"Exactly."

Sex is awkward at best.

What I can deduce from my own meager experience, porn, and Serena's war stories is that guys like to be teased, squeezed, popped until they burst all over you, at which point they're basically deflated hot air balloons taking up the entire bed.

And don't you tell them what you're really fantasizing about is when it will be over and you can take a scalding-hot bath.

"My vibe has more empathy in its first two settings than the guys on campus," I go on, and

Serena cackles. "In fact," I say, lifting my UPenn travel mug, "I may *never* have sex again."

"Noooo!"

Her protest has me laughing. "Plato said there are two things you should never be angry at: what you can help and what you can't."

"Yeah, well. White men who got to wear bed sheets to dinner said a lot of crazy shit." Serena's green eyes slice through me. "Besides. I'm not angry. I'm planning." I raise a brow. "To find you a guy with a tongue that'll turn you inside out."

I shudder. "That's sweet. Truly. But I didn't come to school to get laid, Serena." Her fake shocked face has me rolling my eyes. "I want to do something that matters."

When I started college, my mom told me I was lucky to have been born now, and her daughter, because I'm free to be whatever I want. By that, she meant a famous painter or a rocket scientist, or straight or gay, an advocate for children or the environment.

It's not enough.

Serena's right. I'm obsessed with Jax Jamieson, but it's not because of his hard body or the way he moves or even his voice.

It's because Jax Jamieson *matters*.

He matters by opening his mouth, by lifting his guitar, by drawing breath. He matters by taking people's hopes, their fears, and spinning poetry with them.

Every time I sit down and listen to *Abandon* on vinyl on the floor of my bedroom, a coffee in my hands and my eyes falling closed, it's like he matters a little bit more.

If I ever meet Jax Jamieson, I'm going to ask him how he does it.

Before Serena can answer, my phone rings.

"Hello?"

"This is Wendy from Wicked Records. You got the internship."

Disbelief echoes through me. I glance over my shoulder in case I'm on camera for some reality show. "But what about the other two hundred applicants?"

"Apparently their coffee making left something to be desired. Be here tomorrow at seven thirty."

CHAPTER TWO
Haley

I can't deal with the slippery pants two days in a row, so I borrow Serena's skirt that hobbles me at the knees.

On top of my sleeveless blouse, I stick my leather jacket.

For safety and comfort.

My backpack holds my computer and the completed paperwork HR sent me by email.

Walking through the glass doors should be easier than yesterday—hell, I got the job. But it's not, because I don't know what they expect. I want to ask, "Why did you hire me?" but the security guy checking my paperwork and processing my pass probably isn't the right person to answer.

"You're on two. Up the elevator."

The first two elevators are packed full, so I find a stairwell at the end of the hall.

When I open the door to the second level, I'm in another world.

Pristine carpet, white as snow. Paneled walls in a rich red color that should look retro but doesn't.

I peel off my leather jacket because it's warm up here and glance down the hall.

Wendy's office is supposed to be to the left. But cursing from the first door in the other direction pulls me in.

Inside, a guy who can't be much older than me surveys a computer rig I'd give my leg for. An error message lights up the screen in front of him, blinking like some doomsday prophecy.

"Can I help?" I ask. With a quick head-to-toe that ends on the pass clipped to my waist, he ushers me in.

"What the hell took so long?" the tech asks. "I called IT ten minutes ago."

It's moot to point out that I wasn't with IT ten minutes ago.

My eyes adjust to the low light as the door slips closed behind me. There are no outside windows, just the glass half panel facing the studio and a closed door that connects the two.

Someone's recording in here. The figure in the other room is facing away from the glass, bent over a guitar like he's tuning it.

I push aside the bubble of nerves. My focus is on the computer.

"Is ten minutes a long time?" I ask as I set my paperwork and my jacket on the desk. My fingers start to fly over the keyboard.

"It is when *he's* here."

I hit Enter, and the error message goes away.

It isn't until I straighten that his words start to sink in.

"When who's here?"

That's when I'm viciously assaulted.

At least it feels that way because two horrible things happen in such close succession I can barely tease them apart.

Hands clamp down on my bare arms from behind.

Hot breath fans my ear, and a voice rasps, "What the fuck is going on?"

Every hair on my body stands up, my skin puckering, and I do what any reasonable woman grabbed by a stranger in a vice grip would do.

I scream.

It's not a cry for help.

It's a bellow of rage and defiance. Like a banshee or Daenerys's dragons en route to scorch some slave traders.

Channeling strength I didn't know I had, I whirl

on my heel and collide with a wall. My hands flail in front of me, lashing out at my attacker.

I'm not a puncher, I'm a shover. But when I shove, all that happens is my hands flex on a hard, muscled chest.

I trip backward, my grown-up skirt hobbling me as I fall.

I grab for the desk but only get my papers, which rain down like confetti as I land on my ass.

My heart's racing at an unhealthy speed even before I take in the white sneakers inches from my face.

"Jax. I'm really sorry," the guy behind me says. "I called Jerry ages ago."

Sneakers, as white as the carpet, are pointed straight at me. Dark-blue jeans clinging to long legs, narrow hips. A faded olive-green T-shirt stretches across his chest, like it started out too tight but gave out over dozens of wears. Muscular arms—one covered in a sleeve of tattoos—look like they lift more than guitars.

I force my gaze up even though I want to melt into the floor.

A hard jaw gives way to hair the color of dirt faded in the summer sun. It's sticking straight up in most places but falling at the front to graze his forehead. His nose is straight, his lips full and pursed.

His eyes are molten amber.

Dear *God*, he's beautiful.

I've seen hundreds of pictures of Jax Jamieson,

watched hours of video, and even been to one of his concerts. But the complete effect of all of him, inches from my face, might be too much for one person to handle.

And that's before he speaks.

"I repeat. What. The *fuck*. Is going on?"

His voice is raw silk. Not overly smooth, like the Moviefone guy. A little rough. A precious gemstone cut from rock, preserved in its natural glory.

There are things I'm supposed to say if I ever meet Jax Jamieson.

I wrote them down somewhere.

"I'm Haley Telfer," I manage finally. My throat works as I shove a hand under me, shifting onto my knees to pick up the papers. "But you know that."

His irritation blurs with confusion. "Why would I know that?"

"You're standing on my Social Security number."

One of the papers is under the toe of his sneaker. I grab the edge of it, and his gaze narrows. What is it with me and pissing off these people?

Not that pissing off Wendy comes close to pissing off Jax Jamieson.

(Whom apparently I'm going to refer to with both names until the end of time.)

"Haley Telfer?"

"Yes?" I whisper because, holy shit, Jax Jamieson refers to people with two names too.

"You have ten seconds to get out of my studio."

∾

The tech and I stand next to each other, peering through the glass studio door into the hall. My jacket's back on, not that the guy's coming anywhere near me because he thinks I'm a lunatic.

On the other side of the door, Jax exchanges angry words with a man in a suit.

"That's Shannon Cross," I say.

The tech nods, stiff. "Correct. The CEO showing up means one or both of us is fired."

"Well... which is it?"

We watch as Jax stabs a finger toward me and stalks off.

"I'm guessing you," my companion murmurs.

The door opens, and Shannon Cross looks at me. "My office. Five minutes." He turns and leaves.

After gathering my papers, I take the tech's directions to the elevator to the third floor. A watchful assistant greets me and asks me to take a seat in one of the wingback chairs.

Great. I've been here less than an hour, and I'm about to be fired.

Instead of spinning out, I study the picture on the wall and the caption beside it.

Wicked Records's headquarters. Founded in 1995, relocated to this new building in 2003. Employs two thousand people.

"Miss Telfer."

I turn to see Cross watching me from his

doorway. He exudes strength, but in a different way than Jax. He's older, for one. Tall and lean, with hair so dark it's nearly black. The ends curl over his collar, but I can't imagine it's because he forgot to get a haircut.

His suit is crisply cut to follow the lines of his body. He was one of the men with all the gold statues in the picture yesterday. Yet on this floor, there are no pictures of him.

Weird.

He's made millions—probably billions—in the music industry. Formed stars whose careers took off, flamed out. In the golden age of record executives, he's one of the biggest.

I follow him into his black-and-white office, a continuation of the pristine carpet outside. It should look like something from an old movie, but it doesn't. It's modern.

A fluffy gray rug on the floor under a conversation set looks as if it used to walk.

I'm struck by the urge to run my fingers through it.

The photos gracing the walls here are black-and-white, but they're not of musicians or awards receptions.

They're fields and greenspace.

Err, gray space.

"Is that Ireland?" I blurt. "It looks beautiful."

I turn to find his gaze on me. "It is. My father moved here when I was a child."

I wait to see if he'll offer me a seat, but he doesn't. Nor does he take one as he rounds the black wood desk, resting his fingertips on the blotter.

"Miss Telfer, I understand you interfered with a studio recording session. And assaulted one of our biggest artists."

My jaw drops. "I definitely did not assault him. He started it."

I realize how childish it sounds. The memory of it has my skin shivering again, and I rub my hands over my arms. "Technically, he startled me. I was trying to defend myself. Every modern woman should have a knowledge of self-defense, don't you think?"

He doesn't nod, but he hasn't kicked me out yet, so I keep going.

"I know I shouldn't have walked in, but your tech had this 'FML' look I know from a mile away. I know the software. I use it in the campus music lab all the time. There's a compatibility issue with the most recent update, and..." I trail off as he holds up a hand. "I wanted to fix it."

Appraising eyes study me. "And did you?"

I realize Cross isn't asking me about my outburst but what I'd done before that. "Yes. Yes, I think so."

Cross' lips twitch at the corner. "Jax Jamieson is heading out on the final leg of his U.S. tour, and we're short on technical support. We could use someone with your problem-solving skills to back up our sound engineer."

"You're asking me if I want to go on a rock tour?" Disbelief reverberates through me.

"Of course not." His smile thins. "I'm reassigning you to a rock tour."

End of Sample
To continue reading, pick up *Good Girl* at your favorite retailer.

BOOKS BY PIPER LAWSON

FOR A FULL LIST PLEASE GO TO
PIPERLAWSONBOOKS.COM/BOOKS

KING OF THE COURT SERIES

After being dumped and losing my job the same week, the last thing my broken heart needs is a rebound.

A steamy, grumpy sunshine sports romance featuring a woman down on her luck, a star basketball player with a filthy mouth, and a connection neither of them can deny.

OFF-LIMITS SERIES

Turns out the beautiful man from the club is my new professor... But he wasn't when he kissed me.

Off-Limits is a forbidden age gap college romance series. Find out what happens when the beautiful man from the club is Olivia's hot new professor.

WICKED SERIES

Rockstars don't chase college students. But Jax Jamieson never followed the rules.

Wicked is a new adult rock star series full of nerdy girls, hot rock stars, pet skunks, and ensemble casts you'll want to be friends with forever.

RIVALS SERIES

At seventeen, I offered Tyler Adams my home, my life, my heart. He stole them all.

Rivals is an angsty new adult series. Fans of forbidden romance, enemies to lovers, friends to lovers, and rock star romance will love these books.

ENEMIES SERIES

I sold my soul to a man I hate. Now, he owns me.

Enemies is an enthralling, explosive romance about an American DJ and a British billionaire. If you like wealthy, royal alpha males, enemies to lovers, travel or sexy romance, this series is for you!

ABOUT THE AUTHOR

Piper Lawson is a WSJ and USA Today bestselling author of smart and steamy romance.

She writes women who follow their dreams, best friends who know your dirty secrets and love you anyway, and complex heroes you'll fall hard for.

Piper lives in Canada with her tall and brilliant husband. She's a sucker for dark eyes, dark coffee, and dark chocolate.

For a complete reading list, visit
www.piperlawsonbooks.com/books

**Subscribe to Piper's VIP email list
www.piperlawsonbooks.com/subscribe**

amazon.com/author/piperlawson

bookbub.com/authors/piper-lawson

instagram.com/piperlawsonbooks

facebook.com/piperlawsonbooks

goodreads.com/piperlawson

ACKNOWLEDGMENTS

Thank you for reading King of the Court. There was a time I thought Clay and Nova's story could take place in one book. Looking back, I am both humbled and grateful to be wrong.

I loved seeing the highs and lows of them fighting for their HEA. I loved getting to know the Kodiaks and their friends and family. I loved diving deeper into the world of pro basketball.

This series wouldn't have happened without the support of my awesome readers, including my ARC team. You ladies provide endless enthusiasm, cheerleading, and help spreading the word.
Thank you.

Becca Mysoor: Thank you for making me believe that everything is possible and leading by example. I treasure our friendship more than I can say.

Cassie Robertson: Thank you for bringing consistency to my wacky ideas, and for laughing at my jokes in the margins (but only the good ones).

Devon Burke: Thank you for helping polish my stories into their best selves, and for bringing your incredible heart and wisdom to the task.

Annette Brignac and Kate Tilton: Thank you for being in my corner, for seeing what I'm trying to create in the world and creating it with me. Without you, few things would get done and probably none of it would get done well.

Lori Jackson and Emily Wittig: Thank you for taking my random ideas and wacky gradients and making art from them. I'm grateful you still respond to my emails.

Nina Grinstead and the entire VPR team: thank you for your wisdom, support, and tireless effort to help readers find books they'll love.

Last but not least, thank YOU for reading. Truly. Knowing we're living in these words and worlds together is the best part of any gig I've ever had.

Love always,

Piper

Printed in Great Britain
by Amazon